I0830739

Exodus II
Second Edition

A.S. Reaves

Upland Avenue Productions

Never think you are too far gone...

to make a change.

First Printing: 2015

ISBN 978-0-692-53127-3

Library of Congress: 2015953467

Printed in the Unites States of America

Upland Avenue Publishing
www.astrialegends.com

Contents

Acknowledgements

To God: the all -important head of my life and first in all things. I cannot do anything without You.

To my mom and dad: Thank you for your love and support.

To Pastor Darryl and Pamela Ware of Victory Grace Outreach Christian Church: I can not thank you enough for your kindness, encouragement and support that you have showered me with for all these years. You've helped me to continue to press forward against all odds.

Thank you to all my **friends, family, fans and supporters**…you have given me more inspiration and motivation than I could ever repay. To all my friends online and off…Thank you from the bottom of my heart.

Special Novel Dedications:

My Future Husband, whoever you are (Black)

Shana K. (Confit Cassanade)

April Sheris (Cesna)

The chosen few whose aura will forever help me grow, continue to inspire me and for all that you have done for me as well as being there for me…I give you thanks. I cherish you always.

For those who've been around since the first version was re-leased, thank you for sticking around! It's been a long time coming since Exodus was first released in 2007, and it's been an exciting journey! So, why is there a second edition? First, I had a lot of questions about what happened before the events of Exodus and, from the feedback, it was realized that much of the story couldn't be understood properly having started where I did. So Genesis was born. Genesis changed the rules, the playing field, and the final score. In essence, the time between Genesis and this novel release was spent taking the events of Genesis and restructuring the world they were written around. The cultures, histories, timelines and characters all went through a deep scrub, resulting in a much more believable and cohesive world and storylines. Exodus already needed an overhaul, from the first edition feedback, but I wanted to make sure this version was solid and easier to follow. The flavor of the old version is still hinted at here; if you look closely you will find similar scenes and nuances that have carried over, though the context has changed. Even so, you will now have more ground from Genesis and will see the aftermath of those events pour through. The best of both worlds! So, while it's been forever in waiting, I hope you will find it worth the wait and better than the first!

For those who are new to the series, or new to this version of the novel, welcome! I also wanted to make new readers who are coming into it fresh, with or without having read Genesis to, still have a flavorful experience. The introduction will give you a little summary of some of the important events of Genesis, enough to get you through the first couple of chapters. But this novel introduces a new set of characters, enough so that you are able to enjoy the story without having to have full knowledge of Genesis. If you are new to the series, the books are written from multiple points of view that constantly mix and mingle, the further you read. I do this because I feel you get a more well-rounded perspective of all the events as they happen, when you know the motives and backgrounds of everyone involved. It gives you the freedom to create your own perceptions, without being influenced by one single main character. So judge wisely!

With all that said, let us continue the Dawn of Unity Journey!

For more information, visit the official website:
www.astrialegends.com

On The cover:
Dymona Le'Gless and Alexander Percival

Introduction

Genesis Synopsis:

The Astrians are angels of living, breathing color, charged with keeping the galaxy in peace and harmony. Unfortunately, for most of their creation, they have believed that the best way to keep the harmony is to stay within their own spectrums. Only one Astrian seemed to know better than this, and that was Red. Red is the High Ila, head of all Astrians, and angel of Love. Early in the Astrians' existence, Red created a protective layer around the planets' most susceptible to SIN, the first of which was Zanali. This protective layer is much like the Ozone Layer of Earth and is visible during Aequalis at night. It looks like an iridescent bubble and serves to keep SIN, and its manifestations, out. She knew that if SIN ever had access to Astria and the Astria Galaxy, they were not united enough to overpower it.

All SIN can currently do is send down its messengers and indirectly try to tempt those that dwell within, winning souls for the underworld. Unfortunately, this caused SIN to go on a personal vengeance against the Astrians themselves. Because of the discord among the Astrians, SIN has slowly been corrupting them, until the day that it planned to fight them face to face, something it has never done in the years both have existed.

SIN divided itself into its first manifestation, the seven deadly sins. One sin focused on each of the spectrums, except for Red's. SIN knew Red was smart, so it rather decided to possess the heads of the other spectrums to turn against her, thus causing her fall from power. IRA, though, while keeping her eye on the Spectrum to which she was assigned, also began to tempt Red into succumbing to the evil trait that she represents.

When Red is confronted by all those who are now possessed, and sees her daughter, pink, in a pool of her own blood, she finally loses it, allowing Wrath's temptation to bring about the evil within her and she lashes out. She fights the possessed versions of her once friends and loses. This causes the ripping of her pure heart and her fall from grace. The absence of Red causes those in her court to fade away and because of her connection to the whole of the spectrums, their world begins to cave in.

The Spectrums' corruption by Sin is then complete…and it destroys itself.

Prologue

Around dark eyes bright lights violently crashed into one another, ripping clouds into pieces, shattering what was once so quiet and peaceful. Rainbows spilled colors like blood, giving the skyline mixed signals and the wrong reasons to shine. The SINs had finally corrupted one of the most sacred places in the Astria Galaxy and only emerald eyes were left standing, quiet and solemn, but not defeated.

Just like it was in the beginning.

And now she doesn't remember me.

As he watched, his head shook slightly, as he never thought he would see the day the sky cried. All he could do was watch, as his eyes shifted one color to the next, mixed emotions creating the same tidal wave inside of him, as the SINs did to this world.

She doesn't remember anything.

He was sitting on the edge of a tattered cloud when he saw it: One by one, those with the power to see the spiritual world, lost it, and every trace of the colors vanished, now limited to the skies highest depths, awaiting the day to shine again.

Maybe she remembers something.

He was left, surrounded by only what was there in the beginning, the essence of himself. In the midst of the chaos, one large eye materialized on the horizon. The eye was outlined in silver and edged with golden spheres that glistened brighter than the light of the sun. The eye opened to reveal a pupil filled with a deep magenta and a midnight blue catlike slit in the center. It appeared to scan the world as it gave off a light red glow before the eye slowly closed. The red glow radiated brighter and poured into the skyline, engulfing the eye in its wake. Moments later the glow dimmed, until it vanished, leaving no trace of its visit.

Maybe this is my chance…

Figure 1 - May I help You?

Original Background photo courtesy of Kiran Dambala.
Used with permission.

1 – Stuck

"The greatest loss is when we find our place in life, our purpose, and the place where we truly belong… right before we lose everything." Various Authors. <u>Quotes of the Ages</u>

⇛⇝⇛⇝⇛⇝⇛⇝⇛⇝⇛⇝⇛⇝⇛⇝⇛⇝⇛⇝⇛

As the suns settled in the sky, the rainbow patterns melded together to become nothing more than a light tint of blue. A blanket of snowy clouds came to crowd around the unsuspecting yellow balls only to cover their many rays of light. A few rays were able to poke between the masses of trees and shine down onto the surface. The trees stood proudly, lining the landscape like soldiers protecting a prized possession. There in the middle of the trees, lay a woman, completely lost in thought. Her shoulder length black hair, with red highlights, mixed with the blades of grass, as her pink eyes gazed up through the trees. Holding onto a thread of memory, an incomplete thought, she tried her best to remember the rest of it. She scanned her surroundings, hoping something would trigger the answers she sought. As she moved to sit up, a pain shot from her lower back, all the way to her head. A quick hand cradling her head was the only thing preventing her from toppling back to the ground. Her head continued to respond in throbs, the more she pressed it, to unlock the memories she knew had to be there. It was to the point she couldn't even remember how she wandered into this forest, or how long she'd been asleep. She closed her eyes, waiting for her mind to stop spinning. It never did. Reluctantly, she pulled her body from the ground, and slowly and unsteadily, headed towards the shoreline. The woman was glancing out into the crimson waves, far across the horizon, silently praying to the Exalted One, when she saw it. Hovering almost straight across the water, the vision's magnificence glowed against the sky. It appeared like the smoothed over dissection of a sequoia tree, by the size, and the wood of it a stunning mix of browns. The surface of the wooden tablet housed a group of unfamiliar pictures one would think were an alien form of hieroglyphics. It floated in midair across the water, over unfamiliar land, its face slowly turning clockwise. She stared at it for a while, recalling the fact that this was the third time in a single week it's appeared, and always in the exact same place. As she watched it fade and disappear, she couldn't explain the strong urge to find it.

How can I find something I'm not even sure exists?

She thought, her eyes still fixed on the spot where it vanished. She smiled, her twin fox tails swaying casually as she started towards the water. Prying her eyes away, she kneeled down to let her hands slip into the cool waves, as she gazed at her reflection.

How could I even find my way across the water?

Her restless eyes finally settled on a deep blue, as she focused on the soothing movements of the waves. She enjoyed the tranquility of staring through the water, almost in a trance. Unexpectedly, the next moment found her soaking wet, on her back, as a large long necked creature broke through the water in front of her. The massive creative caused waves to crash against her and almost drag her into the ocean.

"HEY!" she sputtered, coughing, and rubbing the water away from her eyes. Before she could mutter any more words of anger at her attacker, the shadow of the huge creature covered her, while one, multicolored, crystal-looking third 'eye' radiated from the top of its head and pointed right at her.

May I help you?

She heard it speak into her mind, its voice was musical and somewhat familiar, but her shock at hearing it froze her own thoughts. It tilted its head slightly and repeated itself.

"D - did I invade your space?" she asked, not knowing if the creature had intentions of having her for dinner.

"No. You called me."

"I... what?" She frantically shook her head, trying to understand. "I don't even know what you are, how could I..."

"You called me. Just now. May I help you?"

The woman gawked at the creature for what seemed like forever as she slowly crept to her feet. Careful not to be perceived a threat, she pointed back towards the ocean, "Do you know any other lands this ocean leads to?" she asked, in a mouse-like whisper.

The creature nodded its large head. *"I know these waters well."*

"Could you take me across?"

"I AM NOT A RIDE!"

Its head was now only a few inches away from her. She threw her hands up and backed away. "Sorry, could you at least point me to the nearest land away from here?" She pointed in the direction she'd seen the vision and watched the snow white neck of the strange creature turn to look.

"The land you point to is Korin, straight across."

"Thank you," she responded, taking a deep breath before diving into the water. The creature watched her for a while, noticing she wasn't the most graceful creature in the water, nor very fast.

Exodus II

"It will take her forever to get to shore at that rate." It said to itself, chuckling a bit at the way the woman fought to stay above the water. After a while the creature groaned under its breath, shaking its head, before diving into the waves. Its three long peacock tail feathers fanned the waves with expert precision. A moment later the woman felt something lift her up out of the water. The shock almost caused her to roll off, back into the waves, if not for the gentle words: *"It's just me, hang on."* The woman rubbed the water out of her eyes and then reached around to hug the neck of the creature.

"Thank you…" she started, "but I thought you weren't a ride…"

The creature shook its head again. *"I couldn't stand another moment of watching you try and swim. You'd never make it."*

"Well, I was doing my best!"

"That's why I couldn't stand it. What's your name anyway?"

The woman had to think for a moment, before the name came to her. "Legna." It sounded like her name, but at the same time it didn't. As she spoke it, the name seemed empty, like a vessel devoid of life giving water.

"I am Cesna."

Legna noted that the water bird's name had the same emptiness to her. "Can I ask what type of creature you are, Cesna?"

The creature smirked. *"Yes you may."*

Legna wasn't amused, but almost huffed, "Ok, what type of creature are you?"

"I am a Yaitali."

"A real Yaitali! The great water bird! Wow, I'm honored."

❦❧❦❧❦❧❦❧❦❧❦❧❦❧❦❧❦❧❦❧❦❧❦❧❦

There was one continent, or inita, which no one dared to explore, the inita of Zavare, where the zavi made their home. The land changed as they populated the area, causing it to decay. Lush grasses lost their color, shriveling up and fading away, while dried up rocks from the mountains surrounding the inita, took over the landscape, changing to a ghostly, dull, bluish tint. Far different than a desert, the ground was hard as concrete to the touch and no amount of water could bring life back to what was long gone. The zavi built their homes right into the mountains, until they were nothing more than a mass of interconnected, dark, creepy caves. Beneath these caves, accented by leftover water runoff from the mountains above, were the dungeons. Placed deep beneath the mountains, within the darkest, dampest places to be out of sight and out of mind.

Deep within the dungeons, in a single solitary cell, was Ambrose. Outside of the dungeons, his name was never mentioned, a silent taboo, just as if he never existed. Dymona was the only one who'd take the time to go through the hidden catacombs to visit him. The dungeons were heavily guarded, both at the entrances as well as near each cell. Dymona always had a hard time getting in; the guards would taunt and search her just for the mere pleasure of it. She'd become just as much of a spectacle as Ambrose, a fate she'd only wish on Zephyrus. Deep down she couldn't help but harbor a distinct hatred for the man, though she knew his actions were common among their race. Even so, she struggled daily to fight the hatred she felt for him and for the zavi ways in general. The last thing she wanted was for it to engulf and control her again.

Exodus II

Ambrose was kept in the furthest cell from the entrance of the deepest dungeon, not only confined by steel bars, but also a constant wave of electricity that connected the walls of the entrance to his cell. Dymona was not allowed inside the cell with him to visit, nor would the guards give them any privacy. The most they would do is leave the sides of the cell, while still remaining within earshot to continue laughing and taunting them.

It was hard for her to see Ambrose's appearance. By now the gashes left from his broken wings were scabbed and healed as best as could be expected in his current condition. His eyes were sunken and weary; being held in a confined space was taking its toll on him. They both knew the Sire had no intentions of ever releasing him. The biggest wear and tear on Ambrose's spirit was the fact that he went through all the trouble to manipulate an innocent woman into causing total chaos for his sake and he didn't even get on the council. And to make matters worse, he was starting to regret the entire thing. Dymona would try her best to comfort him, but to no avail. The only subject that would get him to smile would be talking of their days in the catacombs, before he was caught. Ambrose had to admit, the past few weeks taught him a lot and he now knew the truth in her words.

When Dymona wasn't sneaking off to visit him, she'd stay in her room or within the catacombs. She made herself as invisible as she could, and had gotten pretty good at it. She'd also taken to reading the book she received from the Astrian. Knowing that the Exalted One still heard her prayers and responded to them, she was inclined to pray every now and then. It still wasn't a comfortable feeling for her, but she earnestly wanted to understand what love actually was. It was the main thing she would pray for, or what she thought was praying. She didn't really know what she was doing, and with no one to ask, she just hoped that her feeble attempts would be enough to one day receive an answer. The more she did so, the more she felt something urging her to get outside the walls of the caves and catacombs, and away from Zavare altogether. Today, she decided to do it. Tucking the book tightly in a sack, she strapped the sack snugly to her waist. Leaving her room, Dymona moved silently through the dense fog covered floors, until she wandered near the cave of the Sire and nearly got smacked by Zephyrus, as he flew down the stairs. Being very curious natured, she leaped up into the rafters, scaling them with ease, moving from one hanging rock to another, as she followed him. She found him gathered around a group of zavi in heavy armor.

"The Sire is still restless. He has not forgotten that you failed your previous mission," Zephyrus began.

"He is restless, or are you?" one of the other zavi mocked. "It doesn't seem like this woman is of any real concern to him."

"You don't know what's on the Sire's mind!" Zephyrus snapped, "I am being held responsible for your mistake and I will not have your failure tarnish my record! You will go and dispose of the serenda, and this time I'm going to personally see that you don't fail again!" The hunters turned on their heels and stormed out, leaving him standing, gritting his teeth. Dymona was frozen on the spot, wrapped around a long piece of rock. Part of her wanted to rush and tell Ambrose, but the other part wanted Eva dead. Was she still filled with hate? Or was it love? She wasn't sure. She watched Zephyrus follow the others out, after taking the time to cool down his temper. As her mind thought about the possibilities, another voice seemed to add its advice to her thoughts. She heard a rumbling shrieking sound, and turned to see an unfamiliar, green-eyed zavi, standing behind her.

"Who are you?"

"It's such a shame." She spoke, her voice echoing with each word. "That girl, Eva, is causing so much trouble."

Exodus II

"That isn't telling me who you are. And you're wearing a green uniform, you aren't even in my clan."

"I can understand how you are feeling right now, though," the zavi continued, ignoring the comments, "She's the only thing standing in your way."

"In my way of what? And how can you understand anything? I don't even know you!" Dymona growled, back flipping off the rock she was wrapped around.

"You really should help them kill her," she continued, "Then there would be nothing standing in your way." Dymona folded her arms and turned her back on the zavi. The female zavi stepped closer. "Don't you want that attention? Don't you remember how you felt, when he dressed up all nicely, just for her?"

Dymona's arms loosened a bit. "You don't know what you're…"

"He probably kissed her and held her close." Dymona bit her lip and the zavi's green eyes flashed, becoming more vivid, honing in on Dymona's heightening feelings of jealousy. The shrieking noise could be heard again. "Without Eva, Ambrose would turn his affection to you."

Ambrose.

The name broke through her madness. She blinked. She hadn't factored in any of his feelings. Dymona shook her head. She knew she couldn't bear the sight of Ambrose any lower than he already was. And even if she decided to go ahead and tell him of their plan, she couldn't free him. So what could he do?

"CRAP!" she gritted her teeth. "You have got to be kidding me." She groaned, shoving past the woman and heading towards her cave. "I…am going to have to save her myself." She stopped at this revelation, still groaning to herself. "Well, I said I needed to get away from this place. I guess I got my wish." She gave a heavy sigh, as she reached her small cave and quickly gathered up her belongings. The zavi gave a last look at the place that was her comfort for so long, before heading out the door.

"We shall meet again." The green eyes zavi sneered, walking through the caves and out into the light. Her shadow reflected off the outer rocks in a large disjointed shape that didn't match her form. She grinned, watching Dymona until she was out of sight before disappearing in a cloud of green smoke.

2- Getting Away

"It is in our darkest hour that we need those who believe in us, so we can believe in ourselves." <u>Penumbra</u>

As Legna and Cesna moved towards the coast of Korin, they watched the suns set over the horizon, casting amber and golden reflections onto the water in front of them. When Cesna felt her foot hit the sands on the shore of Korin, both breathed a sigh of relief.

"Oh, my butt is so sore!" Legna sighed, as she hobbled off the massive water bird's neck.

"Rather just your behind than your whole body. I swam this entire way, don't forget. I did all the work." Cesna moved her long neck, until her head was right above Legna's.

"I was going to say thank you!" Legna defended, as she tried to straighten up. There was a harmony of popping, as each joint voiced its relief.

Cesna leaned back and tilted her head. *"Do you always make noises like that?"*

Legna laughed. "Only when I've been in one position for almost an entire day." She yawned and looked up. "Speaking of, I should try to find somewhere to sleep for the night."

Cesna tilted her head the other way, *"Do you even know where you're going? And why did you want to come here any-way?"*

Legna looked down, mulling over her thoughts, then her eyes glanced over to the yaitali. "As crazy as it sounds, there's a relic that I feel I must find. It's been plaguing my dreams, ever since I found myself in the deserts of Mati. Lately, visions of it have overtaken my waking moments as well." She turned her head, gazing out over the uncharted lands before her. "I don't even know if it exists, but if I don't try, then I'm afraid it will drive me insane."

"But why here?"

"This is where I saw the vision, hovering over the water."

"You are right. It sounds totally crazy." Cesna yawned and cast her eyes back towards the water. *"I'm way too tired to swim back now. How about we just camp here for the night?"* She didn't wait for Legna to respond, before sniffing out a thick, sandy spot near the shore. Legna, not having any better ideas, simply followed suit, watching Cesna sniff the area three times before curling up in a ball. Her tired eyes barely opened to see Legna and, without a word, the enormous bird lifted her tail feathers as an invitation. Legna, yawning, crawled over into the ball Cesna made and curled herself under the thick feathers of her tail and both soon drifted off to sleep.

Legna's dream wasn't different tonight. It was one that plagued her nights, as much as the vision of the wooden tablet did her days:

Her dream took her to the clouds, where a new world opened up before her. Her eyes filled with a magnificent red, as was the elegant dress that adorned her. It was long, with gold bands lining the ends and decorated with red hearts, gold gems and sparkles. A ruby tiara lay softly upon her head, which matched the ruby shoes on her feet. Silver ribbons on the belt of her dress played in the wind, as she sat upon the moon, overlooking the universe. She sat among the clouds, while wondrous spectacles of purple, blue, and pink danced across the heavens that enveloped her, along with glittering lights and planets, whose presence creat-

ed auras all their own. She was in the midst of true splendor, with a feeling of belonging, but at the same time, was distant from it. Then all went black.

In the midst of utter darkness, like a void smothering her, so thick it was hard to even breathe. She was suspended in midair on her knees, doubled over. With all the fancy garments gone it was just her, alone again. At that moment her gaze lifted, to meet a massively huge figure she'd never seen before. It encompassed every color of the rainbow, but the colors were dark, dull, and reflected the negative aura that the figure radiated. Hauntingly azure eyes pierced the black and caused her body to tense. She found herself without words, without sound and almost immobile. The closer it stepped, the more the pain stung in her shoulder blades. The pain grew and stung deeper, not only on her shoulder blades, but down into the deepest parts of her, causing her to lose her breath. Her lips parted, taking in the bitterness of the air, as he slowly moved closer, her hands clinching with the last of the strength that she could find.

It won't end like this!

She yelled and with that vow in her heart, she screamed. The scream ruptured all that it hit, it broke the darkness, shattering the image before her and dissipating the blue, until all was overshadowed by a blinding, white light.

The white light again, am I more than I believe I am?

❦❧❦❧❦❧❦❧❦❧❦❧❦❧❦❧❦❧❦❧❦❧❦❧

The oceans covering the planet moved like liquid fire, as the crimson waves washed over shore upon shore, making a distinct break between the coast of Zavare and that of Kaatina. Kaatina was named after the first illura that inhabited the area: Kana Umbre. Though she was the third ruler of the Esailles Regency, she was known as the last of the just rulers. She was beautiful and fair, always wanting the best for her people. After her passing, the Percival family took over but Kaatina continued to reflect her everlasting beauty. The continent was a vast meadow full of flutterflutterbies and bunniflies. From the Shrouded Forest to the Crystal Lake, there was an abundance of flora, fauna and its own special wonders to keep the memory of Kana alive. In the midst of Kaatina's meadow stood many small buildings, reminiscent of rounded Indian teepees. They were placed strategically, to form a large, crescent moon shape, if looked at from overhead. The tips of the moon marked the houses of the guards and greeters of the clan and in the middle of the moon stood the royal palace, where the Prime and Prima Sai lived.

Some called this regency, the guardians of the night because their True Illura were blessed with the influence of shadows. They could morph the shadows, move seamlessly through them, become one with them and twinkle like the stars in the sky. This gave many the wrong impression, saying that they were evil beings, simply because of their gift. Normally, this interpretation would be wrong, but the Percival Family line aimed to fit that description perfectly. Currently, the Percivals are in their ninth generation of rule, with Alexander Kali Percival, the son they called "the problem child".

Prime Sai Percival was 6'2" with long, black hair that shined like silk. His dark mocha skin made his light brown eyes sparkle. The single 's' curl which hung in his face, only added more definition to his hard look, along with his strong cheek bones, and clean cut mustache. He was usually seen in a form fitting, white, collar shirt, with short, puffed sleeves, under a maroon vest and black pants.

Alexander accepted the throne under the mass speculation of the other illura. He hadn't exactly proven himself within his family line, nor had he gained the cruel influence over his people that his family expected of him. Alex was no pushover though; he had a very short sporadic temper and those who even eyed him wrong, could face brutal punishment. There was even hostility and tension between him and his wife, Yeve. Even so, the history of his family line gave him enough intimidation, so that no one dared question anything he did. Unfortunately, the majority of the populace still believed he was emotionally unstable and a threat to the throne, even if they couldn't put a finger on why.

The only one who was anywhere near close to Alex, was Stevan, one of his most loyal sentinels. He had a quick wit and sharp tongue that could talk him out of almost any situation. Short for an illura, at only 5'4", he was mostly overlooked by the other nobility and mistaken for a weakling by the others, even though he passed all the training and was a full-fledged sentinel. Alex found that the boy had a keen ear, very agile fighting skills and knew when to just smile and nod. Stevan proved himself to be reliable, dependable and, more importantly, trustworthy. It was for that reason he kept Stevan close, rewarding Stevan by promoting him to an elite sentinel, which allowed him room and board in Esailles Palace. By being an elite, Stevan got to view the brain behind the instability of Alex and secretly held a deep respect for him. Though there were still times he felt confused and intimidated by Alex's behaviors.

This was one of those days. Stevan viewed the Prime Sai from the doorway of the main throne room within the palace. It was large and the light blue floor tiles chilled his bare feet. Darkness filled the room, so much, that the bitterness of it was the only flavor the room carried. A dry wind, trapped between the walls, blew across Stevan's face and the bundle of short, icy blue hair on his head, shifted at its touch. At the far end of the room, a lone throne stood. It was tall, black and made of a leather-like material.

Exodus II

It was facing the wall and a tiny glint of light shone on each side. On this wall was a small hole, where the light could travel through and mix with the never ending darkness that instantly swallowed it, keeping the room dull and gloomy.

"Prime Sai Percival..." Stevan said softly, not wanting to disturb the thick silence. At his words, the throne slowly turned around to face the door, with a squeak that echoed off of the walls. Stevan cringed at the sound. He sat there, his eyes matching the stillness of the room, his hands clasped loosely on his lap. He gazed over at Stevan and then at the man he was holding. His brown skin darkened, as Stevan's grip on his neck tightened. "What am I supposed to do with this one?"

Alex sighed, as his figure rose from the throne. His cape flowed down behind him, as he made his way up to his sentinel. His steps echoed like thunder, as his shoes hit the linoleum. "What did he do?" he asked, his dark eyes creeping from Stevan to the guy.

"Repeated disrespect to the Prima Sai," he answered.

Alex groaned at this, walking around the two slowly. "Let me guess, she wants me to honor her dignity?"

"Yes, she requests his death." Stevan paused a moment. "He is also a True Illura."

"A fellow shadow walker. I am surprised she doesn't want him as a slave." He stared into the man's eyes. "What's so special about you?"

"Nothing." The man gulped.

"His name is Terrin," Stevan informed, still watching his leader.

"The Earth Journalist." Alex bemused.

"You know about me?" He stared up at the Prime Sai.

"Now, why would a journalist intimidate her so?" He posed to himself, ignoring the question.

"Excuse me, sir?" Stevan interrupted, puzzled. "What was that?"

He cleared his throat, resigning himself once again to what he believed was his fate in life. It was the same routine, but this was the first time his wife ever requested him to do her dirty work. Normally, she'd hire zavi to do her bidding, in exchange for helping to increase their numbers. He figured it must be one of her puppet shows. Of course, he was the puppet. "Very well." He took the guy from Stevan's grasp digging his fingers into the man's skin. He reached underneath his coat, pulling out a navy blue dagger, whose hilt curved around the sides of his hand, as he held the base. Its blade dimly glinted in the darkness, casting reflections on the sapphire stone in the center of the hilt. The blade created a small arc of light, in reaction to his fluid motion, and made a clean slice of the man's throat. He let go of the body and it crumpled to the ground with a low resonating thud. He took another long look at the fallen man. He had eyes of coral, with short hair to match, the ends dipped in black. On his arms there were a few coral spots, near the wrist of his left hand that looked like freckles atop his camel brown skin. He turned away quickly. "Stevan, you are dismissed," he said sternly, as he stepped back to his throne. Once Stevan shut the door, he turned back to the hole in the wall. He looked out into the light, twirling the piece of wall in his fingers. The light burned his eyes, but he couldn't turn away, constantly longing for freedom.

3- The Little Thief

"The smallest package may hold the greatest key to your deepest desire." Various Authors. <u>Quotes of the Ages</u>

✥✥✥✥✥✥✥✥✥✥✥✥✥✥✥✥✥✥✥

"Come back here you little thief!" a feminine voice yelled angrily, breaking the silence in a span of around a mile away from where Legna and Cesna were sleeping. A creature ran at top speed, away from the sound of the voice, like darkness cutting through the light. He scampered across the grass as if his life depended on whatever was inside the leather pouch he was dragging along in his maw. "You'll wish you never stole that bag when I catch up with you!" the woman yelled, shoulder length silver locks blowing in the wind behind her. She was carrying a sword, like a baseball bat, ready to hack the first thing that interrupted her path. She kept her eye focused on him, poised to strike the little critter as soon as she got close enough. Seeing the duo sleeping ahead, he darted straight for them dropping the bag near Legna's head before jumping behind her, and hiding between her and Cesna. The smell of the bag's contents made it to Legna's nostrils and her eyes opened, responding to the strong growl in her stomach caused by the smell.

"Mm…" she took a long inhalation as she yawned. "What's this bag doing here?" Her stomach growled again. Looking down at the bag she started to peek inside when the creature's pursuer finally caught up to them.

"So! You are the cause of my misfortune!" the woman exclaimed, pointing the end of her weapon at Legna. She was tall and pear shaped, wearing an old dusty green peasant top under a pale orange corset tank with a pair of worn orange pants. Around her head hung a thick green cloth, tied in the back and completely covering her forehead. Her large fox ears stood straight up and a long raggedy tail trailed behind her.

In the light of having the end of a sword just a few inches away from her nose, Legna dropped the bag, "I don't even know what you're talking about!" She folded her arms. "For your information I was asleep."

The woman's eyes narrowed and she moved the weapon closer. "Don't play stupid with me thief! Sending your little henchman to steal my hard earned food! Did you think I wouldn't catch you?"

"What henchman?! And what part of *I was asleep* don't you understand!" She eyed the leather bag again, and picked it up. "Oh this must be what you're worked up over." She threw it at the woman's feet, "There, you have it back."

The woman just kept staring at her. "That rat hiding behind you," she stated still disbelieving Legna's story. Cesna, who'd been shaken awake by the commotion, took the woman's words personally and opened her eyes.

"*I am no thief and I am not hiding,*" she said plainly, lifting her large head and staring back at her.

Realizing that what she'd mistaken for a large rock was in reality a living being, the woman quickly backed away, dropping her weapon in the process. "I...I wasn't talking about you..." she stammered.

This made Legna actually look behind her. "Oh! What do we have here?" she smiled, picking up the little creature in her arms. He looked like a mini dragon, with fluffy jet black fur all over, except for on his underbelly. This fur was snow white. His eyes were like onyx, but reflected glows of every color, while silver dragonfly wings sat upon its back. His ears were of odd shapes, almost like flower petals or leaves. He also had a long, bushy black tail with splotches of white. "It's ok little fella, I won't hurt you."

"You won't hurt him, but I will," she warned, snatching her sword from the ground.

"You got your bag back so clam up will you? There's no need to harm him, he's probably just as hungry as I am." This statement was met with another stomach growl.

The woman tilted her head. "That really isn't your hench-man?"

"No…" she replied exasperated. "I told you, I was sleeping. I've never seen him before, in fact, I only *arrived* here last night."

Cesna suddenly looked back out towards the waves. *"I am sorry but I must go now."* She turned back to the woman. *"I take it there will not be any **problems** once I am gone."*

The woman sheathed her sword, folded her arms and huffed, "Fine. I will leave her and the little thief alone."

Cesna moved her large head close to the woman and her multicolored eye shone brightly. *"You are wise not to. Do not let me find out something has happened."* With that, the massive water bird rose. *"Xetos Legna. We shall meet again."* Her blue eyes flashed as she said this before submerging herself in the crimson waves.

"Xetos," Legna whispered, momentarily forgetting the others. The word gave her a strange sensation like she'd heard it before, but she knew she hadn't. It was only when the little creature shuffled in her arms that she was forced out of her thoughts.

The woman was still sneering as she snatched up her bag. "Lucky little thief, you will live for another day." The woman turned to walk away.

Exodus II

"Hey wait!" Legna turned her attention to the woman. "Who are you anyway?"

The woman stopped and turned her head. "Why should I tell you?"

"Because you interrupted my sleep, threatened me with that sword, and called me a thief. The least you could do is tell me who the heck you are!" she raged, standing and facing her. The creature scampered up and perched on her shoulder.

She thought about this for a moment, before turning back around. "Fine. I am Ni-Prima Sai Katimeria Yani of Metayale."

Legna gaped, "Ni-who?!"

The woman sighed, shaking her head. "You really aren't from around here. You can call me Ni-Prima Kyani." She folded her arms, "I am royalty. The youngest daughter of the late Prima Sai Lana Anari."

Legna chuckled, raising a brow, "If you're royalty, what are you doing out here? Shouldn't you have everything done for you and live in some fancy high class castle somewhere?"

Kyani's eyes narrowed more. "Yeah, I should, but I left the castle long ago."

Legna stepped closer. "Why'd you leave?"

"It's none of your business!" she snapped in reply her eyes flaring at Legna.

"Ok, ok! I get the message." Legna's stomach growled again and this time loud enough for Kyani to hear.

The princess sighed heavily, defeated in her attempts to rid herself of the two. She couldn't leave them alone now or else her conscience would get the best of her. "You might as well come get something to eat," she stated, starting to walk off again.

Legna's eyes widened. "What?"

"I said come on!" she yelled, never stopping to even turn her head, "and you can bring the little thief with you!"

⚜ ⚜ ⚜ ⚜ ⚜ ⚜ ⚜ ⚜ ⚜ ⚜ ⚜ ⚜ ⚜ ⚜ ⚜

Stevan met Alexander outside, and for a moment, the young sentinel watched his master staring blankly off into the horizon far away from Kaatina. Maybe it was regret for the murder he'd just committed, or mulling over the life he had chosen; Stevan didn't know. All he noticed was his master becoming more and more distant, solemn, and leaving the castle for long extended periods of time, for no reason at all. "You can't go on like this..." he said putting a hand on his master's shoulder. "Disappearing without a trace," Stevan added as he pointed to the tear in Alexander's white shirt, and plucked a small twig from it. "Only to return even more distant then you were before. Is there something more interesting out there?"

"I can do as I please..." he replied, snatching his arm away from his sentinel's grip. His mind was blank, spanning far from the situation at hand. His eyes zoned out as if searching for some kind of light in the darkness. Most Esailles Illura loved the darkness and embraced it. As Kana would say, it was 'the true energy of the soul where only the brave could dwell'. Alex, however, was starting to hate it.

Stevan crossed his arms taking a step forward to be in his sight again. "Where have you be running off to?" Stevan asked.

Alex turned to him, balling his fist impatiently. "And what gave you permission to be in my business?"

"I never said I *had* permission," Stevan answered, throwing up his hands. "I just worry for your safety. There are many who would kill to be where you are." He turned away, muttering under his breath, "your wife, for instance." He paused, then speaking in his normal voice he added, "You know, faithful sentinels normally do care."

Alex grunted, "Yea, yea. Point taken." He walked back inside the castle, with Stevan close behind. Within his throne room stood a pale oak table, where he picked up a long coat and proceeded to put it on. It was a deep cerulean blue with long sleeves that draped slightly as they reached his wrists. The Esailles symbol shown in the center of a pattern of white snow-like designs nestled in lighter blue on the upper back of the coat. He lightly brushed his long hair into a ponytail letting his locks fall like night down his back. Having given himself a moment to cool down his temper, he slowly turned back to Stevan with an intense look in his eyes. "Don't you think I know what I am?" He said in grief. "I know very well my state; I have lived in this my whole life…"

"You don't like it?" Stevan interrupted, glancing at the one he looked up to.

Alex continued to look at Stevan as he said this, then moved to pick up Ziay, his small dagger and put it in its sheath. "There has to be more…" he said, almost in a trance. "Besides, nowhere does it say I have to be stuck in these dull walls all day long. I can come and go as I please." He turned back and eyed his servant, waiting for a response. Stevan said nothing. Alex's head lowered, as he took a long breath. He tried his utmost to live up to the leaders of the past. No matter how hard he tried, he just continued to be farther from them, so different in emotions and mannerisms.

"I heard that the Prime Sais before you never ventured past Kaatina," Stevan added suddenly.

With a somewhat downhearted sigh, he said, "Well, if you hadn't noticed," he looked over at Stevan again, "I am NOT the other leaders." And with that he slammed the door behind him.

He walked away from the palace and out of sight. He didn't stop until he reached the forest that occupied the far south east of Kaatina. The reason no one knew where he went off to, was because he hid a small row boat in the mix of trees and bushes and used it to travel beyond the shore of Kaatina to the beautiful forests of Eagali. The suns were slowly creeping down into the horizon as he stepped foot on Eagali, and the light hit the trees in the distance making intricate patterns on the grass below. He stood, letting a small smile creep onto his facial features, as he took in the beauty of it all. Walking through the fresh blades of grass and into the forest, he allowed his mind to blank out and rest from the toils of his burdens. It took him a few hours to travel there and the effort of the journey finally caught up to him. Alex soon found a comfy spot and sat among the grasses, scanning the surroundings for any odd movements. He soon drifted peacefully off to sleep.

Figure 2 - Confit Cassanade

"Could we be like a color? Do we all possess a light shade and a dark shade? And to choose one to live by, does that mean we couldn't change shades if we wanted to?" Various Authors. <u>The Philosophy of Color</u> ~

When she was offered to join Kyani for a bite to eat, she never expected to be hanging upside down from a tall tree. "Is this really necessary?" she asked, trying to reach a large blue tinted flower hanging on the very edge of a branch.

"If you want to eat it is," Kyani stated, sitting back and munching on the now cold contents of the sack. "And I told you to bring that little thief with you, make him help," she smirked, getting a lot of amusement from Legna's predicament. The creature, which was curled up near the base of the tree, perked up at the suggestion and quickly scampered up the tree. He hopped onto the branch Legna was trying to balance on, causing it to sink.

"AAh! No! Get away! You are going to make it break!" Legna screamed, as the creature used its long tail to grab a hold of a nearby branch, still trying to help her reach the flowers. By now Kyani was in fits of laugher at the pair, almost choking on her food. "What are these things anyway?!" Legna yelled, resting from the exertion by hanging upside down by her knees.

"Those are sakro, the petals, when cooked right, have a scrumptious, sweet, nutty flavor, which makes dandy candy."

"Did someone say candy?!" a doe exclaimed, practically skipping into the area. She was a deep mocha with long honey blond hair with green streaks. Her eyes were light brown and she wore a tan peasant top with a mix color, brown corset and wide flared legged pants.

"Confit! How do you always manage to appear anytime someone mentions sweets?"

"Well it is my favorite thing!" she beamed, turning her attention to the tree. "Are we making… " her words were cut off as she spotted the two failing at procuring the flowers. She put her hands on her hips and yelled sternly, "Ni-Prima Sai Katimeria Yani! Are you making a mockery of innocent people again?"

"I don't know what you mean," Kyani responded, folding her arms resentfully at the attitude her full name was being spoken with.

"You know exactly what I mean." She added, reaching in one of the long pockets that lined the sides of her pants.

"Don't you dare!"

Confit paused for a moment, turning to look back at Kyani with a smirk, "You may be royalty, but you don't rule over me. I'm not an illura." She poked her tongue out at Kyani then resumed fishing in her pockets. Legna had managed to sprawl across the branch, staring incredulously at all the flowers. Confit yelled up to her, "Hey! You up there!" Legna looked down at the golden eyed deer. "Let me show you how you are supposed to pick those." Taking two sticks out of her pocket, she effortlessly jumped up to grab a low branch and swing herself into the tree.

"How did you do that?" Legna asked, watching Confit leap from branch to branch, until she was on the one right above. The little thief moved onto Confit's shoulder, sniffing at her curiously.

"I think your little friend wants to know the same thing."

"Little THIEF!" yelled Kyani, who was still watching from below.

Confit laughed. "Still leaving your rations out, where the critters can get to them eh?" She just stared in response, which only made Confit laugh more. "You never learn, and you never listen." She turned her attention back to the task at hand.

"I can't believe you are actually going to help her," Kyani added rolling her eyes.

"Oh, stop being such a stick in the mud. Be sweet for a change. Remember, you never know when you are entertaining angels."

"I used to be nice, long ago," Kyani muttered lowly to herself.

"Come on, up on your feet."

"You're kidding, right?" Legna asked, holding the branch she was wrapped around, as if her life depended on it.

"Yes, I mean it." She kneeled down and began tugging on her arm. "Oh, don't be a baby. You want to eat, don't you? These branches are like rubber, they will bend a lot but they won't break." Legna closed her eyes, allowing herself to be pulled up. "Open your eyes, crazy girl! I'm not going to let you fall!" When she focused back on Confit, her eyes were brown and glimmering. Confit shoved one of the sticks into her hand. "Sugar sticks to sugar here," she taught, while Legna inspected the stick she was given. It was whittled away at one end, so the inside could be seen. "It's pure sugar cane. Now, watch." Confit performed a few expert twirls of her cane, before aiming at the base of a flower. The stick stuck to the base and with a pop the flower came off. "Since the trees grow so high and the flowers only bloom at the very tips of the branches, another sugary plant is the only way to grab them."

"Now that you've told her the secret, could you at least let her work for her meal?" yelled Kyani.

Exodus II

"No, you have worked the poor girl enough already." Confit answered, gracefully swinging from branch to branch knocking down flowers. Legna wobbled from her branch but managed to hit a couple of flowers before the two climbed down from the tree. The creature hopped off Confit's shoulder and back onto Legna's. Confit walked around gathering the flowers they'd knocked down then settled near the already boiling pot of water to pick all the petals. Legna and Kyani also moved to help.

Kyani glanced at the creature. "That little thief seems to really like you."

"Yeah I guess you're right." Legna smiled, glancing over at her shoulder.

"You should name the little guy." Confit gestured, as she put the petals in the pot to cook. "It doesn't seem like he is going anywhere."

"He has a name. THIEF!"

"That is not a name."

"It fits him though."

"I don't even know what he is," Legna interjected.

"Now that you mention it, he looks almost looks like a dragmora but I've never seen a jet black one before. Matter of fact, he seems mute as well. Normally dragmoras are really chatty."

"Hmm… maybe I'll just call him Bandit." Legna chuckled, as the creature nuzzled her neck. "Awe, I think he approves."

The three laughed, as they finished cooking and cooling the candy, then the trio settled down to eat.

"So, Legna, I've been curious," began Kyani. "You said you'd only arrived here this morning. What brought you to Korin?"

Legna swallowed a bit of candy with a large gulp. "Well, I'm sort of looking for something."

"Oh! A scavenger hunt! Sounds exciting, do tell!" Confit exclaimed.

Legna waved her hand dismissively. "I'm not even sure it exists."

"Well, what is it?" asked Kyani.

"It's some kind of wooden tablet with writing and symbols on it."

At this Kyani dropped the piece of candy in her hand, her eyes wide. "A wooden tablet with writing and pictures?"

"Yeah, something like that."

"But how do you know about it?" she asked, her focus glued on Legna, "and how'd you know it was here?"

"In a vision." Legna shrugged. "And I saw it over the ocean above this inita."

"So wait," Confit put her hand up, "You know what she is talking about?"

"Yes I do, and it's odd that even we illura don't know what it is, or where it came from, to say it's on our land."

∾∾∾∾∾∾∾∾∾∾∾∾

Dymona reached the edge of Zavare and looked out towards the crimson waters, out towards the world she never had any interest to explore. Sensing her presence, a magnificent yaitali broke through the waves near the shore. A yaitali is a huge water bird with a long flexible neck and a beak that curls up at the tip. Its three thick tail feathers spanned further than its body length which enabled it to swim with great efficiency. Although it is deemed as a water bird, it is unable to fly as it has no wings. Yaitali are also loners by nature and it takes a great deal for them to trust anyone besides another yaitali. Dymona was granted the trust of one and to this day she isn't sure why. She smiled, wondering if the beautiful bird of the sea would move its home to accommodate her absence. She petted her one true companion for a moment before climbing up on its back. Then she steered the yaitali towards the open ocean, glancing back one last time at Zavare before the yaitali took to the waves.

When Dymona reached the shore of Eagali, she took a deep breath, mulling over what she was about to do. She climbed off the bird and moved low in the grass; glad that the inita was nothing but forests, where her stealth skills would work to her advantage. Sneaking carefully and cautiously through the brush she slowly made her way forward. First, because she didn't want to be seen, and secondly, she needed to figure out what and how she would survive what she started to think was a suicide mission. The only real weapon she had was a short hollowed out bamboo pole and some tiny needles from an akora plant. These needles, when punctured in the skin, left a sedated feeling all over the body. Digging through the brush she saw a clearing drawing near and caught a glimpse of five zavi. Just as she was about to break into the clearing she heard voices. Crouching, she found a place where she could see and yet stay hidden.

"What do you want, shadow walker?" growled one of the zavi. Looking closer she could see that it was Zephyrus. He faced a man she'd never seen before and the first thing that ran through her mind was what fascination men had with long hair.

"I want you to leave," he stated firmly, his long bushy tail swirling behind him. Dymona was surprised that the man wasn't afraid of the pack of zavi that stood before him. She smiled admirably.

"No chance on that, no pest is going to keep me from my goal."

The man just laughed. "You know we have been through this dance many times before."

"Yeah, and each time I find that I like you even less, Alexander."

Dymona wondered why she never heard Zephyrus speak of this man, whom she could tell got under his skin far more than Ambrose. Then again, he really wasn't one who would gladly share information that would hurt his ever-growing ego.

Zephyrus ushered his four cronies to attack the long haired man, as he himself stayed back with a confident smirk. The four zavi rushed him, but he simply sank into the shadows formed from the surrounding foliage. The four ran through him and into the trees right where Dymona was hiding. She jumped, leaping up into the branches where the four wouldn't see her. Alex reformed, delivering a round house kick that collided with Zephyrus' neck, flipping him to the ground. One of the zavi regained his stamina, pulling out a long blade and slashing Alex's back while he was preoccupied. Alex winced, but never stopped, flipping on his hands, wrapping his legs around the zavi's head and throwing him forward.

Alex stopped to take a breath, not knowing another zavi was sneaking up behind with a blade, ready to stab him. Dymona saw this and quickly reached in her bag, pulling out the bamboo pole and needles. Grabbing a needle and placing it in the pole she aimed and blew. The needle hit the zavi in the base of his neck and he slowly tumbled to the ground. Hearing the sound whiz by his ears, Alex turned to see the zavi fall, and glanced towards where Dymona hid but didn't have enough time to investigate. Zephyrus grabbed Alex's arm, turning to face him and then thrust his knee in the illura's chest. Alex sputtered, as Zephyrus jerked his hair and swung him around. Alex growled, as he was tossed into the three other, now functional, zavi.

Dymona shot two more needles, hitting two zavi before they could get a good grip on him. This time Zephyrus turned back, seeming to look directly at Dymona. She jumped and turned to move to another branch, and in her haste smacked her head into the tree trunk. Zephyrus heard the rustle and started to make his way towards the noise, curious as to who was watching him. Alex took the opportunity to grab Ziay from its sheath. With a massive thrust he shoved the dagger into the zavi gripping him, and twisting the blade, pulled it out. The zavi fell instantly. Alex then gave another round house kick, sending Zephyrus to the ground, on his back. He leaped on top of him, aiming Ziay right at the zavi's throat. Meanwhile, the other sedated zavi slowly rose, still woozy with the effects of the needles.

"Tell your buddies to get out of here. Now." Alex demanded. Zephyrus made a gesture to them and they obeyed. He waited until he knew they were out of sight. "Every time we go through this, I end up able to kill you."

"Then why don't you? Huh? Big shot?" Zephyrus egged him on.

Alex's eyes narrowed. "There is only one reason why I don't kill you right now, for all the hurt you've caused."

"Yea? And what might that be?"

"You don't need to know." Alex stood, giving Zephyrus a hard stomp in the chest. The zavi coughed. "Get up and get out of here before I change my mind." Without his guards, Zephyrus knew he didn't stand a chance and took the hint, limping his way out of the forest. With a heavy sigh, Alex watched the zavi until he was no longer in sight. He already knew where Zephyrus was headed. Straight for his wife, Yeve. Alex shook the thought to the back of his mind and turned to the forest of trees behind him. He wasn't crazy, nor stupid, someone had been helping him and he was going to find out who. Peering quietly and carefully through the trees, he finally spotted a figure, crouched, with her back turned.

Being one of the shadows, Alex, too, was very stealthy and he crept up on her with ease. He found her staring at a spot on the ground, holding her head, waiting for the world to stop spinning. "Are you OK, miss?" Alex said softly, trying not to startle her. Dymona jumped up and turned at the sound but, her dizziness got the best of her and she toppled over. He rushed over and caught her, before she landed. "You should be more careful," he smiled, helping her to a sitting position. He then kneeled next to her.

"Yeah…" she muttered weakly. "My head collided with that tree pretty hard."

"I'll stay around until you feel well enough to walk again." Alex offered. This made Dymona finally look at him. In her condition, she hadn't paid attention to whom she was talking to.

"But, you don't even know me. Why waste your time?"

"Well normally I wouldn't, but you did help me back there. It is the least I can do." He paused, rubbing his chin. "But I'm wondering, you are a zavi; why are you fighting your own kind?"

Dymona gave a weak smile. "Besides having a personal dislike for Zephyrus? It's a long story." She gently touched the knot on the side of her head. "As for fighting my own kind, there's no loyalty among the zavi, not even within the same clan."

"Hmm," he pondered. "What will happen if they find out?"

Exodus II

"Humph." She shrugged. "I'm a traitor already, and I've gotten pretty good at staying alive, regardless."

Alex grinned at this. "Well, you go around colliding with trees and you won't be alive for long." Dymona laughed, then complained about how the laughter made her head hurt more. He chuckled and extended his hand to her, "My name is Alexander Percival."

"As in Prime Sai Percival!?" Dymona's eyes widened. "Why, on Astria, are *you* fighting zavi?"

Alex chuckled more. "I have a personal dislike for Zephyrus." He winked at her. "Besides, I can do what I want."

"Oh." She looked away. "I guess you're right."

Alex held out his hand again. "You still haven't told me your name."

"Oh." She shook his hand. "I'm Dymona Le'Gless."

At this, Alex smirked and leaned back on a tree trunk. "Well, if it isn't the famed Dymona of the Great Death."

She turned completely towards him. "Wait, how do you know about that? About me?"

He smirked. "That isn't important. I'm just surprised to see you on the other side of the fence."

"I am not the person I used to be." She stood, noting that her dizziness had subsided. "Besides, I should be going." She turned away and started to walk off.

Alex jumped to his feet. "Listen, I'm sorry if bringing up your past offended you…"

Dymona stopped and looked back at him. He could see the trouble in her eyes. "It…brought a lot of change in my life." She paused. "Thank you for staying with me. It is appreciated." With that, she looked down a moment, turned, and walked out of sight.

Figure 3 - Ila Red Ambroshia

5- Finding Yoursef

"To be honest, I don't know how you would choose. Some are easy 'no's but others…Can you really judge a book only on its cover?" Kyani. <u>Penumbra</u>

Kyani carried her reluctant attitude into the following day. Not only was she annoyed that somehow Legna knew about the mysterious wooden 'tablet' in her homeland, but wanted to be taken to it. Even though Legna was persistent in her pleading, Kyani maintained her refusal to return.

Confit stared at Kyani. "What has gotten into you?" she gave a long sigh. "Even though something happened that made you leave and you don't want to go back, I feel you can at least tell her how to get there herself and I'll go."

Kyani paused for a long while staring far past the two, "No." She got quiet again, glancing over at Legna, her eyes softening with a sudden look of compassion, "I don't want to happen to her, what happened to me." Her focus turned to Confit, "I may be bitter and strong-willed now, but I am not unfeeling. I may not have appreciated the thie—err *Bandit* stealing my lunch or meeting someone who knows about something that brings back unpleasant memories, but I also don't want to add insult to injury by going back there. For me or for her." Kyani turned on her heels.

"And you are going to walk away? Just like that?" pleaded Confit, refusing to believe she was that scarred. Kyani didn't acknowledge her, but for a moment's pause, before closing the door behind her. Confit looked over at Legna, who had been quiet the entire time. She saw her kneeled in prayer, for reasons unknown, feeling that this situation wasn't really worthy of hard prayer. When Legna finally looked up, her eyes were pink and glassy. She stood still, in total silence, and turned to follow Kyani into the cottage. Confit moved to stop her and was met with Legna's hand. Confit stopped, watching Legna enter the cottage and close the door. She found Kyani staring out of a window at the far side of the room. Still not making a sound she simply walked over to her and embraced her in a warm hug. Kyani jumped at the sudden hug and would have pushed her off, but the embrace broke her. Tears streamed down her face as she trembled.

"You haven't felt love in a long time, have you?" Legna whispered. She felt Kyani's body finally slump in defeat. She nodded. "Is that why you don't want to go back?"

"I was forgotten before I ever left," she muttered, as tears continued to slide down her cheeks.

"Do they know how you feel?" she asked, wiping the tears from her eyes. Kyani just shrugged. "You never told them."

Kyani sighed. "They're too busy engrossed in their love lives to even think about me." She broke free to turn and face Legna, "You think any of them, after all this time, has ever made an attempt to find me? No."

"They never…"

"NO," Kyani stressed, trembling again, trying to hold back tears. "And you want to know why they don't?" she balled up her fists. "Because I'm *cursed*!"

"Cursed?"

"Yes." She pointed to the cloth tied around her forehead. "This curse! My own people won't come near me."

Legna reached for the cloth. "But what's under th-"

Kyani slapped her hand away. "I never take this off. At least, with it covered up, it can't cause more trouble than it already has."

Legna rubbed her hand, "But what is the curse?"

Kyani sighed, annoyed. "The curse is... It is..." she suddenly realized that, while everyone thought it was a curse, no one had ever said what the curse actually was. "I'm some kind of seer. And it's a cursed thing...but I don't know how I am cursed."

"Then how do you know it *is* a curse? What if it's a blessing?"

"How could a third eye be a blessing?!" Kyani exclaimed. "It has done nothing but bring me isolation, sorrow and grief!"

"Maybe that's because you haven't given it a chance. All you've done is silence it, instead of seeing what it sees. It can be a spiritual eye, you never know."

Kyani paused for a long while. "Well, now that you mention it, I haven't." she touched the eye through the cloth. "I guess it is a part of me now."

Legna smiled, her eyes glistening, as she looked around the room, "Ni-Prima Kyani, when was the last time you truly embraced who you are?"

"What do you mean? I am always me."

"I mean, embraced who The Exalted One made you, without hiding it." Legna caught sight of one of Kyani's old tiaras on the dresser. It was beautiful, but the beauty hidden in caked up dust and tarnished colors. She picked it up, blowing the dust off. "Look at this! It hasn't been worn in so long, that it's turned colors." Kyani followed her curiously into the bathroom and watched her carefully clean the tiara back to its former shine.

Exodus II

"I haven't worn that since I was a young teenager."

"Well that's what I mean! It's time for you to be proud of who you are." Legna placed the tiara on Kyani's head and its sparkles reflected all over the room. Kyani couldn't help but smile, until she saw Legna pointing at the cloth. "Be proud of all that you are." Kyani took a deep breath and slowly untied the cloth from around her head. As the cloth fell, a glossy vertical eye shone on Kyani's forehead, its silver flourishes curling along her eyebrows.

"Well?"

"Nothing's happening…" Kyani turned and looked at Legna and it was then the eye opened. In a flash, a bright and powerful light engulfed Legna and blinded Kyani. Kyani flailed trying anything she could to stop it but only in vain. She could do nothing to stop the light.

"What? Where am I?" Legna's voice broke out from within the glow, as it slowly faded.

"Legna, I'm so sorry!" Kyani cried, as her third eye closed again. "I told you it was a curse! I should never have-" Her words were cut short when she saw the figure laying on the ground. "Legna? Is that…you?" The figure now had long red hair and strange halo winged markings on her shoulders. Confit rushed into the room having heard all the screaming. Legna rose to a sitting position holding her head, a thousand more broken memories swirling in her mind.

"That eye of yours is powerful." Legna said. "I feel freer somehow."

Confit stared, wide-eyed. "What happened to you?!"

Legna turned to her. "What do you mean?" Kyani pointed to the mirror, too dumbfounded to speak. Confit helped Legna to a standing position, walked her over to it. When Legna saw her reflection in the mirror some pieces of her memories made sense. Kyani was looking worried but saw Legna smile. "I am not Legna. I am Red." As the name left her tongue, she knew it was right. This was the powerful, name that she'd gone by for ages, the one attached to all that she is. She smiled warmly as her eyes shined at Kyani. "Your eye is a blessing."

❧❧❧❧❧❧❧❧❧❧❧❧❧❧❧❧❧❧❧

Among the smoke covered floors of one of Zavare's many caves a lone zaviess sat. A long corridor surrounded her on either side full of spider webs, dust, and smoke. A few torches let off a dim glow that showed like fog lights in the darkness. The light offered a silhouette of her figure on the wall behind her. With her slender legs curled up on her chest, her head rested upon her knees. Long maroon braids fell in front of her face, shielding her golden eyes from view. Balled up for what seemed like forever, she was lost in thought. Her mind raced daily with questions of her existence, of her past and what she ultimately wanted to do with her future.

What have I become?

Her past was a chilling nightmare that became her reality, opening her eyes to things she was never supposed to question. Her own race, purpose and heart became little more than an illusion in her eyes, and yet she was surrounded by ones making up her illusion every day of her life. And now, even with the Book of Light, she still had questions. So many things it talked about were things she'd never personally experienced. It was her duty to steer others away from those things, not to think about embracing them.

If I am no longer a true zavi, then what am I?

Zavi. A species whose sole purpose is to keep their own species in existence. Most are driven by the very hate that caused them to become zavi in the first place, and the more they bring into their species the more powerful they become. The epitome of an unfeeling race, they go to any means necessary to accomplish their purpose and in most cases succeed.

I don't think I can make myself into that creature again...

Two forms every zavi possesses. One is a normal everyday form and the other, is one most zavi feel is their actual form. The ultima is uncontrollable to some and unpredictable to others. If not careful, a zavi could become so consumed in their hate and anger that it takes control and causes them to go into pure rage: a state most never return from. She was one of the lucky ones.

Humph... so much for living up to my name. Dymona. I used to be high in rank. But was I nothing but a pawn? Is that all we are? Am I the only one that sees this? And, just think it was Ambrose T'Nagare that caused me to open my eyes. The only zavi that truly tolerated me, and to this day, has never once called me a traitor. Dymona laughed. *I still wonder what secret he is hiding.*

They are a species made up of those who turned to a hateful, unforgiving, unholy life and perished that way. They strive to turn others towards their inner wicked ways and then kill them, all to keep their existence.

But as hate-filled, corrupted and truly bizarre he is, I still...

She sighed softly, then, lifting her head to rest it against the wall. Her eyes looked up towards the ceiling, to look beyond it, if they were able to.

Something else added to the false hopes and wasted wishes that make up the better part of my daydreams. The acceptance of a feeling that will not go away, a race I no longer fit in with and a future, that, knowing what I know, seems bleak. So I've accepted this.

Her hand moved to hold her forehead and her eyes closed. The look of pain and frustration screamed from her facial features.

What do I do now?

Silent footsteps. Her eyes opened suddenly, the yellow in them glinting in the dim glow.

They must be looking for me.

She fingered her braids into a bundle and tucked them in her slate blue hood and pulled it over her head. She buttoned the shawl attached to the hood, so her deep dusty green skin was hidden from view. All except for the zavi trademark long skinny tail that opened to a blue point at the tip. Her legs were hidden in a dark blue and black blocked fitted skirt which extended down over her black heeled boots.

Reluctantly, she picked herself off the ground and took a moment to stretch her muscles. She had been lost in thought for a great length of time and every muscle in her body was either tight, or asleep. It was a weird sensation when she stood, one that almost caused her to fall back to the ground, if not careful.

Time to become the traitor in disguise my heart tells me that I am. A fate I may never get rid of. But do I want to be?

6- Standing Ground

❧❧❧❧❧❧❧❧❧❧❧❧❧❧❧❧❧❧❧

"Ok so I still don't get it." Confit carried on, as she trailed behind the two, "First she didn't want to go at all and now she is beating us there!"

Red looked back at her. "It's simple, she's going to claim her rightful place."

"To face my people, curse and all." Kyani added, touching the tiara on her head.

"And lead me to the wooden tablet, don't forget."

Kyani giggled. "Yes, of course."

Confit still looked confused. Red wrapped her arm around the woman and explained, "Being afraid of who you are, even down to the divine gifts you don't understand, will always keep you chained, and you never reach your full potential." She smiled, looking towards Kyani. "But there is an unmistakable confidence in accepting and loving how The Exalted One made you."

Confit pondered on this for a moment. "I guess you could be right there," her head tilted a bit, "but what happened to you?"

"I simply showed her that her curse is not a curse at all."

"What do you mean?"

"Look at her shoulders." Kyani pointed, turning back to the others. Confit glanced down to see the halo winged symbol, and wondered why it seemed so familiar.

Exodus II

"I don't get it."

Kyani folded her arms. "Didn't you say, 'you never know when you are entertaining angels'? Well…here is your angel."

Confit gaped at Red. "You're an Astrian?!"

Red nodded. "Yes, though I don't know why I'm here or why I've been limited as I am."

Confit was still confused and would have continued asking questions but for a loud, shrieking noise, which broke through the air, causing the three of them to cover their ears. Bandit ran up to the top of Red's head and looked into the sky as a massive shadow overtook them. "What in the world is that?" Confit mumbled as a huge figure landed in front of them. Its bald head shined in the light as its head turned slowly to analyze each of them with its six eyes. The six wings on its back snapped into a folded position when its eyes met Red's. Moving its six arms wildly, it moved closer to the woman, causing her to fall back.

"Well, well what do we have here?" the beast mused, studying Red closely. The shrieking noise grew louder and caused her to scream, doubling over and knocking Bandit off her head. Confit and Kyani rushed over, trying to help her back up. "Don't tell me you don't remember me." Red forced herself to look the beast in the eyes and memories of a long battle, fought many years ago replayed in her mind.

"Tentatio," she mouthed, fighting the sounds of the shrieking to stand to her feet.

"Ah, you do remember me."

"Who?" Kyani and Confit asked each other.

The beast grabbed Red in two of its many arms. "But you won't remember me for long." It squeezed more and more, trying to suffocate her with the pressure. "Do you have any idea how it feels to be imprisoned for so long?" Without warning, Kyani's eye opened and shot a pure white beam of light at the very center of the creature, causing it to let out a piercing yell. Kyani screamed too, trying in vain to control an eye she was beginning to realize had a mind of its own. Before she could recompose herself, one of the beast's hands swatted her like a bug.

"Kyani!" Confit yelled, running over to her.

"You would do best to stay out of my way," it hissed. At this point Red was starting to lose consciousness, clawing at her captor's hands. A slash ripped through the air cutting Tentatio right through its middle. The beast screeched, dropping Red to the ground. There in the middle of the air was a tall faceless mass of darkness. Not really solid but not transparent either, it was like the night breaking through the dawn. He stood shielding Red from the beast.

"What do you think you're doing?" it growled, craning its head to try and study the newcomer. The faceless man answered in silence, moving it's mass to clout the beast's head, causing one of its eyes to bleed. Tentatio recoiled, slamming the mass with its mighty wings only to find them pouring right through it, as if it were nothing but ink. The darkness reshaped and with a swipe of its hand, a ball of smoke headed straight for Tentatio's face.

"Hey!" the creature hissed again, as it ducked just in time to hear the smoke engulf its multiple wings. Then it turned just in time to see two more hurtling towards it. Pushing its weight onto its back leg, Tentatio leaned on it, barely missing one. Then it pushed up, rolling its weight, jumping over it. Rolling on the ground the creature found himself dodging a fog of smoke balls. Some of them hit its pale green skin, sticking to it like hot tar, and burning its flesh. "Alright…ENOUGH!" Tentatio shouted, as it connected with the next onslaught, blocking them by covering its body in its wings. Opening its wings again, the bevy of smoke was ricocheted back to the dark figure.

The mass held a hand up and caught the spherical smoke and instantly absorbed the energy back into itself as the smoke mixed with the air and vanished. His moves were quick and yet graceful all the same. As soon as the energy was absorbed he brought his arm back around and with a single forceful swipe extracted the energy in a trail of black ink that ignited the ground around the creature like a suffocating fire. Tentatio roared before vanishing "You haven't seen the last of me! I will destroy you!"

The faceless mass of darkness vanished as well, before any of the three could find out who or what it was. Confit tended to both of the others, deciding it best to just let them regain their equilibrium and strength at their own pace, which took quite a while. Though shaken from the experience, the trio decided to press on to Metayale, since they were almost there anyway. Kyani's head was still swimming, and she was beginning to wonder if her eye really wasn't a curse. Red was mulling over the figure that came to her rescue and disappeared just as quickly. Confit was quiet, paying attention to the two of them in case either collapsed.

"I'm sorry, Kyani." Red whispered, breaking the silence.

"For what?" she glanced to the side, putting a hand to her head.

"For Tentatio." Red glanced up at the dawning sky. "If I could have destroyed it, I would have."

"So you really did know what that thing was?" piped Confit.

The angel sighed. "Unfortunately, seeing into its eyes reminded me." She turned to Confit. "I fought with it at the beginning of creation. I… wanted to somehow make amends for the chaos we'd caused. Tentatio, or Temptation, as you would know it, was a basis of growing strength for SIN. Its physical manifestation made it incredibly easy for SINs to become strong enough to form a body."

"Wait… SIN?" Kyani raised a brow. "You mean, like fear, doubt, jealousy, malice, and those things?"

Red stopped, taking a deep breath, before relaying the painful truth, "Yes. What you think is just voices in your head, or just harmless coincidences, tempting you to commit acts you normally wouldn't, are truly the result of SIN's interference."

"But those are just emotions, right?" asked Confit.

Red shook her head. "They are *Sentient Influences of Negation*. All the sins you named, and many more, each have a true form, much like the monstrosity of Tentatio. Only you will never see that. All you will see is the result of its transformations, changing into what would more easily sway you, hearing the sweet voices in your ear to entice you. We, on the other hand, fight them in the spiritual realm. In true form."

"But, you are an Astrian, can't you destroy them?"

Red cringed. "We cannot destroy what we created."

❦❧❦❧❦❧❦❧❦❧❦❧❦❧❦❧❦❧❦❧

The Esailles Palace was regal in its elegant dome shaped presence. The structure glistened in gold and was lined with a jagged edged fence all around. It donned a large symbol on the top of its dome, which was the same symbol all of the Esailles wore upon their garments. It was a gold crescent moon tipped onto its back, with a silver dagger connecting its two ends and piercing its middle. Finally, in the center of the dagger, shone a navy blue, five point star. Eshe stood in front of the building, clad in a deep purple turtleneck top filled with flower prints that matched the lavender pants, flaring out around her purple heeled boots. She was hiding behind one of the two double doors marking the front of the palace. Her hair accented the soft features of her pale pink skin and citrus eyes. Her thick bushy tail was wrapped around her legs. She listened until she heard footsteps approaching the door. Ducking behind one of the two huge towers that made up the sides of the palace, she waited for the footsteps to pass. When she figured the coast was clear, she poked her head around the side of the building only to find her brother standing there with a perplexed look on his face.

He turned and, seeing her, crossed his arms. "And what are *you* doing here?" he asked her.

"Are you telling me I can't stop by to make sure you're still on the land of the living?" she replied smugly. Her eyes seemed to glitter.

Stevan raised a brow. "Now why don't I believe that?"

Eshe laughed. "Just because we have different views on True Illura, doesn't mean I can't still come and check on you. You are my brother, even if you are part of the Esailles Regency."

"What's wrong with my regency?" he asked, running a hand through his hair.

"You should have stayed in Terralyn, like me. We have the only female sentinels and we believe in cultivating and embracing those who are True Illura."

"Well, we embrace True Illura too, in a way." He nervously scratched the back of his head.

"Yes, as slaves. Or they are slain, if they do not comply with your Prime Sai," she retorted, as she moved from behind the tower around to the other side, facing her brother. She leaned upon the tower, folding her arms as her tail proceeded to curl about her legs. "My regency still talks about you. They think one of your new family members, or the rebels, came and brainwashed you into joining them." She laughed a bit. "Though I know you went voluntarily."

"And you declined to tell them different? Besides, most people have come to fear illura, who have the gifts, ever since the Annihilation. We just make sure that they don't get out of hand again." He raised a brow, his arms folding again.

Her eyes narrowed. "Like your Prime Sai is? He's a hypocrite, if ever I saw one, being one himself." She pointed a finger accusingly at him. "And no, I didn't tell them any different; I let them believe what they like. They don't even know that I come and visit you, and if I told them what I know, do you think they wouldn't start being suspicious?"

Stevan smiled. "If you say so, but I got tired of having to walk on eggshells with everyone I met. Face it, Terralyn is terrified of the true ones."

"We are not scared of anyone!" she explained.

He raised a brow. "Don't you realize that the true ones just take advantage of you?" he said walking over to her, putting the back of his hand on her forehead. "I'm surprised the royal family has any order at all."

"Stop it," she said, swiping his hand off of her. "We are not being taken advantage of! There is a lot of order. Plus, the more good we do, the greater is the chance we'll get to see the Spectrums." She pointed towards the sky.

"And you say *we* are brainwashed." He rolled his eyes. "The Spectrums doesn't exist. That's just some legend those guys tell you so that you won't rebel against them," he added, poking her shoulder.

Exodus II

"I am not brainwashed!" she said furiously. "And I would appreciate it if you would respect my beliefs," she added, crossing her arms and turning her back to him.

"Alright you win." He put a hand on her shoulder and his voice became sincere. "You know I don't like having these types of discussions," he smirked behind her head, "but do amuse me for a moment…what exactly would you see in Astria?"

"You'd see the Great Orchestra, obviously." She turned her head back to him, "And partake in the most beautiful and wonderful music you've ever heard."

Stevan cocked his brow. "Whatever you say," he chuckled. "If you guys want to go around proclaiming world peace and professing imaginary lands, that's perfectly fine with me."

Eshe sighed. "No sense in trying to enlighten you about factual information, it's like me stabbing myself in the foot. There's no point to it." She flicked her hand in his face and turned to walk away.

"You're horrible, you know that?" he added, chuckling slightly.

She turned back to him with a raised brow. "And what's that supposed to mean?" she questioned, turning fully to face him again.

"Nothing." He smiled, not wanting to start yet *another* discussion. "I just know my sister." He paused, taking a few steps back towards the wall of the building. "And I love her…even if she is from Terralyn," he added as he leaned against the wall.

Eshe shook her head. "I'd better get going. I just wanted to visit my brother for a moment. They will be looking for me soon," she said, looking up at the sky for a moment, then back to him. "And I love you too, Snowball," she added and then turned around and started on her trek back home.

7- Heartache

When all the things you have come to know and love can change, would you change it and lose everything, or continue living a lie?" ~Red Ambroshia.
The Diary of Red

Eventually, the trio reached the edge of Metayale. Moving through the village they found the start of the forest of dense trees that led to the castle grounds. It was here that the trio decided to rest. Though the others seemed to relax quite easily, Red found herself unable to. Her body was restless, feeling free for the first time in a timespan she couldn't even fathom. Her spirits were lifted and she could feel the winds of opportunity whistling its sweet melody in her ears. She had to move and seeing how sound the others were resting, she figured she could risk a little fun for a moment. Leaving the others for a while. Red ran, as fast as she could feeling every ounce of wind through her long crimson locks. She sped across the dry sandy ground as if she was skating on top of it. When she gathered enough speed, she leaped into the air, her wings appearing, large full angelic feathers in a gradient from rich red to a bright glowing white, lifting her effortlessly into the air. Her voice, nothing but whispers, floated around her, mixing with the air.

I've forgotten what it felt like to fly. To be one with the sky.

The one thing she'd learned, was that true freedom is not about the avenue but about the mind, body and spirit. She took this as her number one concern, while she reigned over Astria, and made it a point to strengthen her body as much as possible. The clouds, fluffy white with reflections of multiple colors, framed the endless stars. The two moons that surrounded Zanali could be seen in the distance, seeming transparent like ghostly eyes, watching over her every move. Her bright pink eyes glanced upwards, and it was almost like she could reach up and touch the clouds, but she was never high enough.

In mid-air she pushed her body upwards, stretching her hands out above her, in order to do a handstand in the sky. Her angel wings drooped downward, as she lifted her right arm up and pushed her body around. It spun on one arm, as her feathers jerked outward. She closed her eyes a moment, as she turned and stretched out her legs. A light red mist steamed from the outline of her body, circulating around it and reaching up into the clouds. She flipped around gracefully and darted into a batch of trees, now below her, the aura leaving a hazy trail behind her, fading slowly at the tail end. The deeper she moved into the forest, the more she felt comfortable with its surroundings. The moons soon lost their hold on her, as she swiftly moved through the trees.

She felt eyes upon her, but she didn't stop to investigate. Twirling in the air, she folded her arms around her, as well as her wings, letting the aura surround her like a blanket, while she danced around the eyes of her curious audience. They watched her intently, not as prey, but more in admiration. She didn't know what they were, but knew that they were somehow attracted to her aura. Like fireflies, each was barely larger than a finger and ranged in every color imaginable. They had no voice, no appearance, just tiny moving spotlights flickering between the trees.

Turning on her back, she floated backwards, just as her aura obscured her from their view. They moved anxiously, in wonder at her disappearance, and to their surprise, they saw a sudden bubble form, right out of the aura, as if the air around them had suddenly been punched. Red mist blew through the top of one of the trees, leaving it with burned edges. The mist reached the sky and then broke into smoke and vanished. Red lifted her body through the hole made by her aura and then hovered right above it. The essence of Fallen Love then did a front split, followed by extending her body out to be parallel to the ground, looking down at the forest below. Her legs came together and bent under her as she bent her arms towards her legs touching her toes in the air. At the extent of her hands and toes, red mist flashed from the tips and she sent a steady jet of it back into the hole. Then she lifted her legs up and followed the trail. Her audience rustled with shared enthusiasm, as if glad to have found her or knowing something that she didn't.

She didn't know these creatures came to be because of her very essence. She stopped short above them, hovering lightly up and down, with a smile beaming from her caramel brown features. The creatures, in turn, took the opportunity to dance around her. The sound they made was rustling, like hundreds of pieces of cloth flapping in an immense wind, sounding like a torrent of chatter. Red hoped it was a good gesture.

Somehow I feel connected to them, but how?

She thought, righting herself again. Then, with a jolt, she left them, flipping her body down and soaring away from them in the same path she had found them. They watched her, as she left and disappeared in the wake of her trail. She had decided to return to the others, as she saw dawn beginning to appear on the horizon.

෧෬෧෬෧෬෧෬෧෬෧෬෧෬෧෬෧෬෧෬෧෬෧෬

Alex returned to his palace a few days later. As he walked through the double doors, Yeve just glared at him, though her piercing, hazel eyes didn't even make him flinch. He knew Zephyrus had already relayed the message. He stared at her, daring her to say something, even though he knew she wouldn't. She hadn't the last few times he'd beaten Zephyrus in a fight. He continued, never moving, never blinking, but she just huffed and walked away. He sighed a bit and shook his head, turning to make his way to his quarters. He met Stevan down the hall. Stevan looked up at him with a huge smile.

"I don't know how you do it."

"Do what?" Alex questioned, raising a brow.

"Get away with clobbering that zavi, every chance you get." Stevan shook his head. "Your wife was furious when she found out, especially that you pulverized his cronies."

Alex shrugged. "In the end it doesn't really matter."

"What do you mean?"

He shook his head again. "I have a dislike for Zephyrus, but there is another reason why I hate him."

Stevan's eyes widened. "Why is that?" He asked curiously.

Alex turned and gave an icy stare. "That is none of your business, and *never* ask me again," he growled. Stevan jumped back, shocked at his master's sudden change in tone. Alex then shoved Stevan to the side, as he stormed past. Stevan watched his master, as he disappeared into his quarters, slamming the door behind him. Once in the confines of his room he let out a long defeated sigh. Walking across the room he picked up a picture that was situated on a nightstand in the corner. Peering at the photo of his and Yeve's wedding day, he scoffed, purposefully dropping the picture, frame and all. He was oddly satisfied with the pile of broken glass it made.

"Nothing but a lie," he declared, still staring at the mess. Prying his eyes from the glass, he collapsed onto the bed. "Five years and never once have we slept in the same bed." The thought made him even more furious. Alex felt betrayed and trapped. It had gotten to the point, he didn't even know the real motives to his actions. He reflected on his confrontation with Yeve, staring into her eyes, waiting for... what? Was he still trying just to make her acknowledge him? Or had he really grown a hatred towards the zavi that stole his wife's heart? "Stole?" he muttered to himself with a bitter laugh. "I never had it to begin with." Saying those words seemed to pierce him to the core. He'd learned over the years about her power-hungry and manipulative ways, which all but made him numb. She didn't want him, she never did. It was just the powerful position that he held. And he fell for it. He squeezed his pillow between his fists. What had he done to deserve this bad turn of fate? He already despised his family and their past. He already had to live up to the cruel expectations of his ancestors, though he knew, deep down, he was only taking out his pent up anger on his people. His people feared him and now his wife was using him.

He thought about Dymona. He wished he could free himself from his bondage, as she had, but he knew he had his duties. No matter how much of a nightmare his life had become, he still had a job to do.

Figure 4 - The Wooden Tablet

8- *Metayale*

"Trust in the LORD with all thine heart; and lean not unto thine own understanding." Proverbs 3:5 (KJV)

Dusk seemed late in coming, but the trio finally reached the outskirts of the Castle grounds. Kyani looked around, the view instantly bringing back fond childhood memories. "It's been so long since I've been home."

"How does it feel?" Red asked.

"I didn't know how much I missed it until now." She looked around again, "Now the wooden tablet is out here somewhere, it was nowhere near-"

THUNK!

"Oof!"

"I think Confit just found it." Red shook her head, turning back to help Confit off the ground, before inspecting the area she tripped over. "Looks like we have some excavation to do." The area where the wooden stump used to sit above the ground was now covered with tall grass and a variety of weeds.

"I'll be happy to rip away this foliage, after face planting me!"

Kyani chuckled, stopping her before she could touch any of it. "W-haha-wait! There could be poisonous weeds in there! We need gloves."

Confit put her hands on her hips. "And where do you expect us to get some from?"

Exodus II

"The castle, of course," shrugged Kyani, leading the group to proceed on. Soon they came up to the castle gates. They were large and had many intricate details on them, and glistened in gold outlines. At the top of the doors were two dove mascots and orange letters, outlined in silver were the words, *Metayale Castle*, one word at the top of each door. There was a Sentinel guard posted on either side of the gate.

"Who goes there?" one of the guards demanded.

"Ni-Prima Sai, Katimeria Yani," she proclaimed, standing tall.

The guards crossed their swords, blocking her. "It is an offense to claim to be of royalty."

"Especially looking like a mere peasant," chimed the other guard.

"What do you mean by that, you-" Confit was stopped by Kyani's hand,

"I should have you discharged for such a mockery on the royal family." The guards simply laughed, until she pulled the cloth from over her third eye. "I say again, I am Ni-Prima Sai Katimeria Yani and I order you to stand aside, before I have you both beheaded!"

As soon as the guards laid eyes on her curse, they immediately stepped aside. "You shouldn't defile the castle grounds with your curse!"

The trio walked through the gates, as the other guard yelled back, "All seers need to die!"

This made Red stop and turn back towards the guards. "You believe this curse is evil, correct?"

One of the guards huffed, "Most definitely."

"So, tell me something then," she continued, taking a few steps back towards them. "Would the Exalted One stand behind something that is evil? And would His angels?"

The guards laughed. "Of course not! That would be absurd!"

Red smirked. "Then I suggest you watch your mouth." The guards watched in shock as angel wings and a halo appeared on her and her shoulder markings glowed. "Do not judge that which you know nothing about."

Kyani beamed, enjoying the look of fear in the eyes of the guards. Red moved back through the gate, her wings and halo vanishing.

"Question, if those guards didn't want you here, why did they let you through?" Confit queried, glancing back at the guards.

"No matter what I am, I'm still royalty. As a highly trained Sentinel, they are to obey the royal family, no matter what."

"Sentinel?"

"Yes, Sentinels are the illura's first line of defense as well as role models for the men who live here. Sentinels go through twelve years of vigorous training, being taught various ways of combat, a high standard of etiquette and a variety of survival skills."

"That sounds tough," said Red.

"It is, not everyone who starts the training makes it to the end. Anyway, a Sentinel would lose his honor if he disobeyed a request of the royal family."

"And probably lose his life!"

Kyani giggled. "Yeah that too..." She tied the cloth around her head again. "I don't want any more surprises."

Exodus II

"Why do they feel your eye is a curse, anyway?" inquired Confit.

Kyani sighed. "Because of the Annihilation." She stopped and turned to them. "You see, I am called a seer now because of my eye. It used to be deemed as a spiritual gift. There were other gifts that we once called spiritual gifts too. The gift is different for each regency, but for ours it was the gift of flight." She pointed to the top of the castle wall, where the regency crest stood. It was a dove with a bird of paradise flower in its beak. "Those who possessed the gift were called True Illura. Long ago, a group of True Illura turned against our own people and almost made Illura extinct. Now the gifts are seen as curses and, depending on the Regency, True Illura are dealt with differently, but it's seldom positive."

"I don't understand why we tend to be quick to condemn an entire class of people, simply because of the few bad ones," Confit sighed, shaking her head sadly, "It's like we suddenly believe that every single one is bad, as if there isn't bad in every class."

The group climbed the stone steps, to the main double doors of the castle. Kyani placed her hand on the door, and the area around her hand glowed orange and there was a click. She opened the door to find a familiar face in the room, tidying up. Even though it's been years since they last talked, the woman didn't look like she'd aged even a day. "Scriya, is that you?" Kyani asked as the woman turned towards the door. Her bluish black hair fell around her chin and her sepia eyes had a warm glow.

"Well is this little Katimeria?" Scriya smiled enveloping Kyani in a tight hug. Her voice was echoed like a chorus and reverberated off the castle walls. "You ran away so long ago, I thought we'd never see you grace the castle again."

Kyani looked away. "Yes, and I wouldn't have come back now but for my friends here." She looked in Scriya's eyes. "You act as if you missed me."

"Why wouldn't I?"

"It's not like any of you came looking for me." She pushed past her to let the others in. Scriya's eyes followed her. "Do you honestly think we didn't search for you?"

Kyani turned sharply. "Yes. I've never seen anyone. You all were just happy to have the curse out of the castle."

"Oh, really?" Scriya urged, raising a brow and beginning to become aggravated. "Just because you didn't see it doesn't mean it didn't happen." She moved away from Kyani to see her guests. "I need to show you…" Scriya's eyes met Red's. Her voice was caught in her throat, "H…High…Ila?!"

"You…know me?"

"Yes!" Scriya exclaimed, bowing before her, "It is always an honor to see you!"

"But how do you know me?"

Scriya tilted her head at the Astrian, seeming to ponder for a while on something. She shrugged finally. "From a vision, I saw you clearly as The Exalted One told me of your coming."

"She is looking for the wooden tablet," interrupted Kyani, tapping her foot impatiently.

"I've had about enough of you." Scriya yanked Kyani's arm. "I'll take you to it in a moment. I need to show her something." Kyani grumbled but was still dragged out of the room. Taking her into the main throne room, she shoved her in front of the royal thrones. As Kyani reluctantly stared at the empty seats she noticed there was three thrones instead of two. The third one had a dusty old crown hanging on its back. She looked back at Scriya, puzzled.

"Well stop staring at me and go look!" she ushered. Kyani slowly walked over to the throne and found, emblazoned in orange and gold were the words *Seer*. She picked up the crown and turned it around in her hand, her eyes wetting with tears. "Yes that position has been there for you since your sister, Kyna, became Queen." Scriya folded her arms. "Now do you still believe no one even thought of you?" She waited a moment, but received no answer. "I suggest you take some time to rethink your attitude. I will be out in the main garden, showing the others the tablet."

Kyani heard her footsteps leave the room and the echo of the slammed door. She sat in the throne that'd been saved her and noticed how clean it'd been kept, despite the dusty crown. She ran her finger along the edge of the arm rest, as tears slid down her face.

Was I wrong? If they came to look for me, why didn't I see them? Or has my anger really gotten the best of me? All because of my third eye. Have I been walking more blind than even it being covered with the cloth?

She remembered what Red had told her. *My eye may not be a curse.* Her mind traveled to the battle and her eye actually helped. *What curse would help an Astrian regain her identity?* Kyani gently removed the cloth from her forehead. She pondered deep into the roots of her anger now, realizing it felt as if the emotion was washed over her, controlling her, feeding off her. She shook her head at the thought. Even so, she kept wondering just how changed she had become.

⋙⋘⋙⋘⋙⋘⋙⋘⋙⋘⋙⋘⋙⋘⋙⋘⋙⋘⋙⋘

Back in Disme, Zephyrus furiously paced in his room. His eyes were glowing and were all you could see, through the dense smoke that snaked across the floor. His cave rested in one of the more humid areas of the inita, so much that those who were not used to it, could have their breath literally taken away upon entering. As he paced, a shadow formed behind him, and he stopped with his back turned to it, having felt the new presence. He already knew who it was.

"You've failed once again," the shadow spoke behind him. "And all I asked of you was a simple task. At least *I* thought it was simple," it said, in a voice that was strong and deep, almost menacing. Zephyrus turned slowly to meet its long sharp fangs. Its two horns were curled along the side of its face and its skin was rough and bright olive green. He stood at 6'8 and was extremely built. His form covered a good bit of the area in Zephyrus's small room. "I should have known such a simple thing as an assassination would be too tough for you."

Zephyrus gritted his teeth, to keep from snapping; instead he grumbled, "Why do you want the woman killed now, anyway? You got your wish. Ambrose is locked away."

The Sire folded his arms and replied sternly, "If she is dead, there will be no way to destroy the Beast she created."

"You don't even know if that creature is going to do what you want," Zephyrus growled, pacing back and forth. "For all you know, it could go on some rampage and kill us as well!"

"Are you questioning the judgment of the Council?"

Zephyrus flicked his hand. "I'm only *saying* The Council should focus their efforts on surveilling the creature, rather than wasting time trying to kill a useless serenda."

The Sire sneered. "We are not wasting our time doing so, and it is why we gave the task to *you*." He showed his glistening fangs. "If we'd focused our precious time on it, it would have been done the first time."

"Well, excuse me if I have to deal with that stupid Illura every chance he gets to be a thorn in my side." Zephyrus rolled his eyes. "Besides, I thought the Esailles Regency was on our side."

The sire's head turned at the question. "They are."

Zephyrus narrowed his eyes and the glow of them brightened. He scowled, "Well, if they were then their leader would NOT have fought me when I went to kill her!"

"He fought you? He wasn't even supposed to be there," the sire said, stroking his chin thoughtfully.

"All I know is that I am tired of picking up his pieces. He's been trying to ruin this plan from the very beginning." This snapped the sire out of his thoughts and his eyes glared back down at Zephyrus.

"He has nothing to do with your current position." He interrupted, with a harsh, cold voice. "You've lost enough for your past failures…do not lose your title because of it also."

"As if I haven't lost it already. You knew what was going to happen, didn't you?"

The sire said nothing. Zephyrus growled again and left the room. He walked into another dimly lit room, still full of the dense fog that shaded the floor from view. The shattered glass was strewn everywhere. He placed his hand among the glass, letting the sharp edges cut his skin and allow the blood to mix with the fog as both the sensation of heat and pain filled his senses. Picking up his hand he looked at the shards of glass that lie stuck into his skin, the glow in his eyes shifting to black. "He lost his wings and his status because of you…" he said resentfully. "Am I to lose mine as well?" His lips pulled away from his teeth and glimmering fangs were seen as he slung his hand away, letting out a loud growl, as the shards were thrown across the room, almost hitting the unsuspecting zaviess that happened to poke her head through the door.

"Someone seems stressed…" Dymona teased, her voice casual, shrugging off his anger nonchalantly. She leaned against the base of the doorway, her slender, yellow eyes staring at him. He looked at her and narrowed his eyes.

"What do you want?" he demanded.

"Nothing, from you." She glared. "Looks to me like you're the one who needs something."

"I'm actually surprised to see you," he cooed, "I know the others have been looking for you for a few xanas lately. It seems you like disappearing." He smirked eerily.

"That is none of your business. You people are so nosy anyway," she added, as she stepped into the room.

Zephyrus snorted, "We are nosy? Humph, you're the one always romping around me, with your nose so far into what I'm doing, I'm surprised you have a life of your own."

Dymona simply smiled. "Like I said, I feel it is my duty to check on my fellow zavi." She spoke as she picked up a shard of glass and studied it.

"Fellow zavi? More like bother *me*."

She snickered a bit, generally ignoring the comment. "Broke another door didn't you?" she smirked, glancing from the shard over to him. "I didn't even know you could bring them here."

Zephyrus punched a hole in the wall right near her face. "Listen, I'm not like your little play thing, rotting down in the dungeon. I have no problem ripping your head off. So I suggest you mind your own business."

She just laughed again, shoving his arm away from her face. "S'Fine with me. Besides, why would I help someone no one believes is capable of anything, anyway?" She plucked the pieces of wall off of her shoulders.

"What are you talking about?"

"If you would get your head out of the Sire's butt for a change, you'd notice that you're now the laughing stock of the clan." Her eyes sharpened and focused dead on him, as she leaned close. "If I didn't know better I'd say Ambrose has more respect than you do right about now." She shoved him aside and glided out of the room, her head held high, carrying something she'd slipped out of his room.

Figure 5 - The Wooden Tablet

"The Future…is it better to know beforehand? Or is ignorance really bliss? If we see what is to be…would the joy fulfill us, or is the pain sad enough to make us change? Or would it be better for us to never know…" ~Katimeria Yani.
<u>Seeing Beyond the Veil</u>

"Right through this door," ushered Scriya, leading the guests out into the lush garden area behind the castle, "And watch your-"

THUD!

"…step. Are you OK, Confit?" Scriya tried not to laugh, as she helped the girl get to her feet."

"Yeah, I'm fine, luckily this nice grass broke my fall."

Scriya snickered, "Alright, you two, the wooden tablet is over here." She walked across the garden to a spot surrounded by thick round bushes with multicolored flowers. Red stepped between the two, finally coming face to face with the object of her many visions. She placed her hand on its surface. It was smooth and glossy even though the outer edges were still rough and ragged like the tree it used to be. There were a multitude of markings on the slate and the others kept quiet while Red reviewed them. Kyani soon joined them, dressed in a dress more appropriate for her title. Scriya and Red both smiled upon seeing her, before turning their attention back on the wooden tablet.

In the center of the slate stood a replica of the Spectrums, the eight petal flower that was closed like a flower bud. Around it were four figures holding hands, each one having the illura symbol shown on their torso. One of the figures had a large eye scrawled on top of its head. Then around the edge of the slate were seven large coins.

Red continued to move her hand slowly around the slate. "The four must be the gates." She spoke, then glanced at Kyani, "And the one with the eye, has to be you."

"Me?"

"Yes, if I remember correctly, the gates are always led by a seer," recalled Red, "It is the seer who knows which Illura make up the other three gates." She smiled, "I don't know why it didn't dawn on me before; I guess little by little my memories are coming back to me." She then gazed up at the sky. "The Exalted One knew I'd need help in this."

"We always wondered where the slate came from," added Scriya. "It seemed to just break through the ground one day many years ago. None of us could make out any meaning from it." She giggled. "Nathaniel found it one day just like you did Confit. By painful accident." The group laughed.

Red went back to studying the slate. "I don't know what these coins are, but I feel the gates are the key to bringing the Spectrums back. That has to be why it's pictured here."

"Makes sense," chimed Scriya

"But how am I supposed to find the gates?" asked Kyani, looking worried that she wasn't capable of such a task.

Just then more footsteps tracked through the grass. "I heard I needed to come back here, that there was a gathering going on." A cheerful woman giggled, as she moved towards the group. The woman was tall, with camel brown skin and eyes that matched the deep orange gown she wore. A crown filled with citrine jewels sat between her large, fox ears, while long silver dreadlocks fell down her back. The trio along with Scriya turned to the sound of the voice.

Before anyone else could speak, Kyani locked eyes with the woman and her third eye started to glow, engulfing the lady in a bright light. Upon seeing the supposed attack on the queen a squad of sentinels rushed in breaking up the group and grabbing Kyani to try and stop the beam of light, but she was frozen to the spot and though the sentinels were strong, none could budge her. They found it was the same with the queen. Both just stood, showered in an endless white glow. When the light finally cleared, the woman was dressed in a long orange and gold embroidered gown that was open in the back revealing the illura markings that were housed there. Kyani shook herself out of the trance and held her head.

"What happened?"

"We should take you in for attacking the Queen with your..." it was then the King noticed who she was. "Kyani? Is that you?"

Kyani was still blinking, trying to come out of the coma, "Nathaniel? Y...yes it's me...I think..."

Nathaniel threw his arms around her. "We have been worried sick about you!"

Kyani pried the king off of her. "Humph," she grumbled, folding her arms, as her anger and jealousy rose again, even with her having seen the third throne.

"I am really glad that my little sister is home," added the Queen, though still standing in the same spot the light engulfed her in. "But could someone please tell me WHAT IS GOING ON?!"

The group silenced. Red stepped up and smiled. "You are one of the gates."

Exodus II

The queen looked at her. "Gates? You mean that old myth about illura being the un-awakened gates of Astria?"

"It's no myth, and now is the time to be awakened."

"So Kyani's eye…it's…"

"Given to her with the power to find the gates needed now. It is her honor." Red smiled at Kyani, who stuck her tongue out at the queen.

"But who are you?" the queen asked, still confused about the whole situation.

"I am -"

"She is the High Ila! Head of the Astrians!" exclaimed Scriya, flailing about.

"Scriya, please!" Red face-palmed, "It's really not that big of a deal."

Both the king and queen's jaws dropped. "Is it true?" the king asked.

"Yes."

"Well, I'd say it was a big deal!" added the queen. "We should celebrate! I'll get the staff to start setting it up!"

The queen turned back towards the door, but the king grabbed her arm, "Whoa, we should probably understand her reason for being here before we start throwing a party." He turned back to Red, "May we enquire why you have graced our presence?"

Red nodded and acknowledged the wooden slate. "I came to see this. You see, my world, the Spectrums, that surround the planets of our galaxy have been destroyed or closed. I cannot see nor access them. And my powers that came with being an Astrian have been locked as a result. This is the only vision I have had to lead to any direction." She pointed to the four figures. "These are the gates, the ones that with Kyani's help I need to find. Once brought together they will somehow open the Spectrums again." She sighed, "At least I hope they will."

"But where are the other angels? Why is there no one else to help you?" the queen asked, staring at Red with concern.

Red looked down to study the slate again. "I don't know."

❧❦❧❦❧❦❧❦❧❦❧❦❧❦❧❦❧❦❧❦❧❦❧❦❧

Eyes peeked into a dark room lit only by a few sparse candles. The air was cold, clammy and stuffy with the amount of people solemnly gathered around. Five large zavi stood in a semicircle at the far end of the room, their backs to the onlooker. It was the Council, consisting of the largest and most powerful zavi in the land. There was one representative from each of the five clans in Zanali. He noticed that the group had some unfamiliar visitors. Though the Council towered over even the tallest zavi, these beings towered over them. They were the strangest things he had ever seen. Their bodies were disjointed and their hands were sometimes large enough to engulf themselves, with room to spare. Some only had a single eye and no face, some didn't even have a mouth. But they were there, taking up most of the empty space in the room, hovering over the Council like hungry beasts.

"What do you want?" he heard one of the council members say, "besides what we already offer you?"

He heard the beings sneer, their voices bouncing off the walls, almost robotically, "We want you to release Temptation."

The man had no clue what they were talking about, but he was glued to the spot, his curiosity holding him in place. "How do we do that?" another Council member asked. "We don't even know what you are talking about."

Exodus II

The beasts moved around amongst themselves, before a book fell before the five zavi. "In there is what you need to know. Release Temptation and you will have all you ever wanted. You will be unstoppable."

This caused a lot of chatter between the council members that is until one caught sight of the onlooker out of the corner of his eyes. "Hey you! What are you doing here?!"

Chaos broke out as the beasts disappeared through the ceiling and the eavesdropper ran out as fast as his legs could take him. Through the halls and into one of the hidden catacombs hoping that in the darkness they didn't know who he was.

They did.

"Now I sit in a cell." Ambrose sighed, leaning back against the cold wall as he remembered the night that changed his life. "And I didn't get to do anything I'd planned." His eyes narrowed, "I want to know what was going on." He rubbed his temples, "Something about that room, those creatures, it really didn't sit well with me. And I want to know why." He stared out of the bars of his cell. It was pretty quiet now, the guards were off on the hunt and the electric cross bars that gave extra coverage were on for the night. "Nothing has ever affected me like that before." He then thought of Dymona and of Eva. "Well at least, in a negative way." Ambrose sighed again, slumping in his seat. "So many emotions I just don't understand. I wasn't made for this."

Click, clack...

Footsteps...

Ambrose jumped to his feet, looking around, trying to find the source of the sound, but also not adding to the noise himself. He saw the shadow of a figure leap onto one of the low hanging rocks above his cell,

"Dymona?!"

Dymona jumped, almost sliding off the hanging rock, "Keep your voice down, idiot!" she yelled in a whisper. "I'm trying to get you out of here." She pulled out a piece of glass from her bag and slid it through the bars. "Hold on to that."

"A door? Where did you get-"

"Don't worry about that, just be quiet stupid." She was starting to have second thoughts but pulled out a small pickaxe anyway. "I'll break up the rocks and get you out of here," she said, starting to use the axe to drill into the rock.

"You know how long that will take?"

"Didn't I tell you to shut up?" she added, agitated now. "No one asked you to rate my methods."

Ambrose simply chuckled. "Well it's nice to see you on edge, instead of me."

Dymona beat the rock harder. "I could leave you in here, y'know."

"Yes you could, but..." he paused a bit, "I'm glad you aren't." This made Dymona stop for a moment, the hint of a smile showing up on her features, though she was glad Ambrose couldn't see it. She returned to hitting the rocks, seeing bits and pieces of it fall away. Ambrose sat back down and just listened to her work, neither saying another word. After a while, she started to see a pin sized hole leading into the cell and started to get excited.

"Hey! I'm -"

"Ahh Dymona!" Another voice broke their silence, "I thought you might be up to something!"

Exodus II

"Zephyrus!" Dymona screamed dropping the axe. "What are you doing here?!"

"You thought your clever taunting would ensure that I'd be out with the others tonight. Well your brilliant idea didn't work. I never left." He walked over to Ambrose cell and stared in at him. "Trying to break out the object of your affection eh?" he grinned.

"Don't you start with me," snarled Dymona.

"Oh, don't get mad now, traitor, you wait until I tell the Sire. He'd love to know what you are up to."

"You wouldn't!"

"Oh yes, I would. I got him put in there, what makes you special? I may be a laughing stock, as you say, but I'm not traitor." He eyed Ambrose, "And I'm certainly not in a cell, pitiful and weak." Ambrose growled, rushing to the cell bars, forgetting the extra bars and immediately felt electricity course through his body till he was thrown back in the cell. Zephyrus only laughed. "I really don't know what's so special about you." He looked at Dymona. "Both of you are pathetic." Dymona leaped at him from the top of the cell, digging into his shoulders with her claws. They struggled for a while, but Zephyrus tore her off of him with one arm and sent her crashing into the far wall. Ambrose rushed to the corner of his cell to see her, trembling, in an attempt to stand again. Zephyrus laughed and turned to leave. "If I were you, I'd get out of here, The Sire won't like this much, when he finds out." Zephyrus laughed all the way out of the dungeon.

Figure 6 - Watching From Afar

Original background photo courtesy of Kiran Dambala.
Used with permission.

10- Change of Heart

The queen did get her banquet the next morning. The grand banquet hall was lined with silver and gold draped tables filled to capacity with food. In the center of the room the citizens danced to music played by a live band. The King, royal court and the Majestic Circle, mingled with the guests and citizens alike, an opportunity that rarely presented itself. In the mix of the hustle and bustle of the celebration, the Queen was finally able to pull Kyani to the side. "Kyani, why did you leave us that day?"

Kyani huffed, "Didn't you read my letter, Kyna?"

"I did, but…"

"That told you everything you need to know." She looked away.

"All it said was how everyone got their happy endings, but all you got was a curse." Kyani didn't move, "We were too close, for too long, for me not to feel like you are bottling up something."

"Close?" Kyani snapped. "Once Nathaniel came into the picture, I was a stranger to you."

"Kyani, how could you say that?!"

"Don't play stupid with me. You replaced me, just like that. All the time we spent together, you replaced it with trying to sneak out with him. You never had time for the one person who truly looked up to you."

"You…looked up to…"

Exodus II

"Sure, you came by and said, 'Hi' occasionally, but all you talked about was him." Kyani grabbed her hand and dragged her up the stairs to her old bedroom. "I could no longer confide in the only person I felt comfortable talking to."

"But Kyani, I didn't kn-"

Kyani reached under her bed and pulled out an old dusty book and threw it into Kyna's lap. "Do you have any idea how it felt to be the little sister?" Kyna pored through the pages, reading her sisters doubts and fears, her thoughts on Kyna's own past suitors, and her journals that revealed just how alone and hopeless she felt.

"Sister, were you really that lonely?"

Kyani slumped her shoulders, "I couldn't help it. No one wanted me because I wasn't you. I wasn't heir to the throne, so I was invisible. Then when you replaced..."

"Stop saying I replaced you! I did not replace you, I love you."

Kyani glared. "When was the last time we spent time together before, I left? And I mean the last time you made time for me, when it wasn't just to talk about him, or when he wasn't available?" Kyna thought for a moment but couldn't answer. "I thought so. You don't just drop people you love and think about them when it's 'convenient'."

Kyna was silent for a long time, she had no idea what she'd done until now. Her sister was telling the truth. She had gotten what she always wanted and completely disregarded the one person who loved her unconditionally. "I'm...I'm so sorry Kyani." She put a hand to her head and closed her eyes. "I had no idea. Is there any way to make it up to you?"

"No. My childhood is gone. I made it by myself." Kyani folded her arms and turned away. "You got your happy ending, and I hope you are satisfied."

"But..." Kyna pleaded, but then glanced up at the ceiling, "We did come to look for you. Multiple times."

This made Kyani turn her head. "You...did?"

Kyna looked at her. "Yes, but every time we got close to Nauti, we were attacked and could never get through."

"I don't believe that. We have some of the strongest sentinels in the land."

"Yes, but whatever it was we were fighting, didn't take to our weapons. We lost a lot of lives back then." She looked to the floor, then glanced away.

It was then that Red walked up to them. "I think it's about time for us to head out. We still need to find the other two gates."

Kyani peeled herself from the wall. "This is true; we should get a move on."

Red looked at Kyna. "You will have to come with us."

"What?!" both Kyna and Kyani said in unison.

"You are one of the gates, so you need to be there when we find the others."

The two followed Red back down into the main banquet hall where the King was waiting for them, "I've arranged for your absence, my love. Go where you are needed."

Kyna smiled at Nathaniel and embraced him, "Thank you my king."

"Be careful, love." The King bowed to Red. "I've also arranged transportation for you all."

Exodus II

"Thank you. I'll miss you." Kyna stared up into her love's eyes and smiled. "Behave yourself."

The king laughed. "You know I will." He cupped her face in his hands, "And I'll miss you too." Kyna wrapped her arms around him as he leaned closer to her. His lips pressed softly against hers, as his fingers ran through her locks.

"Oh, come on!" Kyani interrupted, tromping through the hall and out the double doors. "We could leave if they pry themselves off of each other!" She hollered.

Red raised a brow at this, following behind her, leaving the two lovebirds to their goodbyes. She passed by Confit and noticed she hadn't moved. "Aren't you coming?"

"Nope." She shook her head. "I figured I'd stay and help out around here, while the Queen is gone."

"Are you sure?"

"Yes, I think I'll be more helpful here, than on the journey with you all. It seems all I'm doing at the moment is tripping over things." They both laughed.

"I hope we meet again," Red added, giving Confit a hug.

"I'm sure of it." She nodded, watching Red continue towards the exit. On the way, she reflected on the warm embraces of the King and Queen. In the time that she'd been regaining her memories, the sight of them reminded her of someone. Someone she used to know. The only one she used to love. Silver. Their breakup replayed in her mind. The moment where she realized just how much he'd changed towards her. Where he used to be supportive, was now like pulling teeth; her dreams became his joke; and for all the ways she'd tried her best to make him happy, seemed dull in his eyes now. They'd been together practically since the dawn of creation and she never thought she would ever be alone again. She knew that he was the one. But now, facing the realization that he wasn't, made her sick to the stomach. How does one go on, when you find out the one you've poured your heart into, trusted and loved, with your all, for more years than you can count, isn't the one for you?

⁕⁕⁕⁕⁕⁕⁕⁕⁕⁕⁕⁕⁕⁕⁕⁕

Alex, Stevan and Amal were outside, on the very coast of Kaatina. Amal was a sentinel in training, whom Stevan found had a lot of potential. He was a foot taller than Stevan, with short wavy teal hair and slate blue eyes. He wore the sentinel training uniform in deep red and blue with black sleeves. The two had decided to do a bit of practicing near the ocean. Stevan managed to somehow convince Alex to join them in their sparring match, something Alex would never be caught doing. But Stevan noticed lately he seemed to be doing a lot of things he normally wouldn't. Amal helped by reminding Alex of his position and how much of an honor it is to gain insight from him. Being that most of his subjects had varying degrees of negative to fearful opinions about him, Alex figured it was Stevan's coercing that led up to Amal's sudden interest in his fighting skills. So there he was, standing between the two younger illura, with a quarterstaff in hand, defending himself from their staffs. Surprisingly, he found the exercise refreshing, and laughing at the young Amal being thwarted to the ground, was an added bonus.

Meanwhile, Dymona had taken to the waves, spending time with her Yaitali, Cesna. The water bird dove into the crimson waves, taking Dymona with her, so that both moved gracefully beneath. Cesna's head popped back up, with Dymona balanced on top and she lifted her high into the air. It was then that she spotted three figures on Kaatina's shore, one being very familiar to her. She slid down the bird's neck and balanced on her back focused on the sparring trio.

Exodus II

"Are you ok?" Cesna asked, noticing the zavi's shift of attention.

"Yeah, just…watching," she answered softly.

Cesna turned her head in the direction Dymona was facing and saw the object of her attention. *"Does that man interest you?"* Cesna asked. *"He was the one from the fight on Eagali right?"*

"Yes, he was. And very different for one of their kind. At least from that regency."

Cesna laughed. *"One could say you are different from your kind as well."*

She grinned. "Actually, he did. But I still don't understand why he helped me. He doesn't even know me."

"I wish you'd get off the 'don't know you' thing. He knows you now. Get over it. Besides there is this thing called kindness." The yaitali slowly crept closer to Kaatina's shore, taking the small hint that maybe the woman might want a better look. Alex was now balanced on the staff, with his legs curled around Amal's, chuckling at the boy trying to break it free.

"You are going to break your weapon like that, child," he warned.

Stevan laughed. "If you break it you owe me. I made it for you!" Alex released the weapon, swinging his legs around before landing on his feet again. Stevan caught sight of the two travelling closer, out of the corner of his eye. "Hey, looks like you have an admirer, Prime Sai."

"Oh?" he asked, his back turned to the ocean, he and Amal still batting staffs.

"I'm serious, though she is still quite a distance away." Stevan grinned, taking the opportunity of his master in such a pleasant mood.

Alex chuckled, "I don't even know who you are talking about." He jabbed Amal in the side with the staff, ducking Amal's staff as it twirled over his head.

"Well you could always look!" Stevan flailed, getting hit by the other end of Alex's staff.

Alex finally turned to see Dymona watching them, from about a third of the distance away from the shore. Amal took the opportunity to try and clock him on the head with his staff. Alex grabbed the end of the quarterstaff just before it made contact, sliding his staff around, and colliding with the back of Amal's legs. The boy fell over backwards and landed on his butt, letting go of his staff, to break his fall. Alex let go as well, so the staff fell on the boy's chest. Alex never took his eyes off the two, "Hmm..." he whispered to himself, before turning to Stevan, "You need to teach Amal the art of stealth." He then threw his staff into Stevan's hand. "So, take over." Before Stevan or Amal could speak a single word of protest, Alex dove into the water himself.

"Where'd he go?" Dymona asked, not really expecting Cesna to be able to answer.

"He probably saw you," she joked.

"That's really not fun-" Her words were cut off, as a second Yaitali broke through the water, showering the two in the process. Alex was balancing on the bird's neck.

"Did anyone tell you it's not nice to spy on people?"

"ALEX!" Dymona screamed, almost jumping off Cesna. The yaitali shuffled, to counter her surprise.

Exodus II

"Careful there," she piped in.

Alex chuckled, "Care to tell me, to what I owe such an audience?"

"I was just watching your footwork, I didn't know illura were so trained." She shrugged.

"Yes, at least I try to ensure that my sentinels are able to defend themselves," he explained, knowing full well that was one of the rare times he'd actively trained anyone.

"Well it seems like you're doing a good job of that." As she spoke those words, Alex moved further along the neck of the bird, closer to her. Dymona immediately pulled Cesna back away from him. "What are you doing?"

Alex laughed again. "My, you're jittery for the zavi that commenced the Great Death."

Dymona huffed, "I'm not used to people getting so close." She eyed him. "Remember, I kill for a living."

Alex raised a brow. "You also run head first into trees."

Dymona tried not to respond, but couldn't help but giggle at the way he said it.

"He has a point there…"

"Oh, you hush!" Dymona poked the side of Cesna's head. Alex joined in the laughter, as Cesna recoiled and knocked Dymona off into the water.

"Poke me, will you."

Alex jumped in the ocean after her, just as he saw her head bob above the water. She saw him coming and splashed water at him. "I don't need your help!"

All Alex did was continue to laugh. "You really aren't used to kindness are you?"

"I told you."

"Didn't I tell you to hush?"

Alex mused, "What is she saying to you?"

"Um… it's not important."

"Your friend seems to not know of kindness." Alex's yaitali spoke to him. Alex thought about this long and hard, as he watched Dymona climb back onto Cesna's back. Kindness was the last thing he was ever known to show to anyone, and yet here stands someone who didn't even know what it was. And while this entire day was different in more ways than one, his lightened mood allowed him to toy with the idea of showing her what kindness really felt like, even if only to watch it make her squirm and feel uncomfortable. He continued to think about it, as his yaitali lifted him up out of the water.

Maybe it's time for a change. In more ways than one.

11- Hidden Fire

Red was still in deep reflection, when the group made it outside. There in front of the castle, stood one of the King's main carriages. The carriage itself was a deep amber, outlined in gold and silver, with the Metayale crest hanging over the door. Pulling the carriage were four stout moustells, which looked like horse-sized mice. On their heads were thick antlers on which hung small glistening stones that jingled in the wind. When the four ran together their antlers collectively filled the air with music. Red declined to enter the carriage but the other three did. Red flew above it, giving herself more time to think alone as they traveled. Confit repeatedly tried in vain to get Kyna and Kyani to talk to each other. Kyani merely groaned in response and Kyna stared at her in silence, still mulling over all she'd said. So the group rode most of the distance in complete silence until they noticed the land drastically change the nearer they came to the shore and the city of Nauti. Red landed in front of them as Confit urged the moustells to stop.

"Whoa, what happened here?" Kyani pondered as her eyes scanned their surroundings. "We were just here a few days ago." The land seemed far more dried up than a desert should be, to the point that no amount of water could restore it. Most of the sand had vanished and only handfuls of the tiny sandy grains remained, sprinkled about. The group slowly continued on but it seemed the land only became more deformed the closer they got to Nauti.

Exodus II

"This is around the area my troop got attacked," added Kyna, scanning the horizon for any sign of movement. "Though the land didn't look like this."

Red halted suddenly and touched the ground. The carriage stopped and the others got out to take a closer look as well. "This land has been corrupted." She registered what Kyna said. "Attacked by whom?"

"MMuuumfh!!!" yelled Kyani, as a hand went over her mouth, the other around her waist, dragging her away from the others. Another figure immediately tied a cloth around her head, covering her third eye. The group turned towards the figures, seeing three more near the two handling Kyani. They looked like illura, in green and gold attire, but you couldn't see their faces for the thick hoods they wore. Kyna rushed at the two figures, holding her sister, but she hit an invisible shield and landed with a thud. "We can't allow you to stop our feeding," one of the hooded figures bellowed.

"Feeding?" Red asked. She was still trying to focus on what was going on. She saw the figures, but to her they looked odd. She felt there was something inorganic about their appearance. In the distance she could also see a faint, disjointed silhouette watching the group. A ghostly shadow gaining strength directly from land, or so it seemed. Staring more, she realized that the figure was Tentatio.

"Could you help over here?!" shrieked Kyna, barely fighting off two men. Red snapped out of her thoughts, leaping to Kyna's aid while Kyani struggled with her captors.

TWACK!

Red was hit in the back of the head by the third man and she fell to the side. Her vision blurred, as she trembled to sit up. She could feel the man's foot digging in her side. If she could only focus. Nothing made sense. She quickly glanced back out towards the ghostly, disjointed onlooker and was surprised to see the dark faceless man fighting it. She blinked again and both the figures were gone. She thought she was just seeing things from being hit in the head. Red grabbed the man's foot and yanked it off of her, causing him to lose his balance and fall back. Red struggled to get back to her feet, seeing Kyna losing her battle.

"You are just as useless as you were back then," the man behind her groaned. "No wonder the Spectrums died at your hands."

Red snapped, turning to the figure and grabbing him by the neck. The figure just laughed. In her fit of rage, her hand became hot, and fire leaked through her skin causing him to stop laughing and start screaming. "I am not useless." The other men fighting with Kyna stopped at the sound of the screaming. As Red's anger and frustration grew, so did the fire, until she felt some familiar paw pads climbing up her back, to her shoulder, and licking her face. "Bandit!" she giggled, "Now you stop that, this isn't the time!" The fire faded, as she dropped the man, her momentary rage fading with it. Bandit leaped from her shoulder and scurried across to Kyani, ripping the cloth from around her eye, before the men could put up their shield. "Kyani! Your eye! Focus!"

Kyani closed her eyes as her third eye started to glow. Kyna and Red didn't see anything, but heard all the figures screaming, falling to the ground and squirming as if they were being tortured. Then the figures faded into the air and were gone. Kyna just stared. Kyani's third eye calmed and closed, then she opened her eyes. "W…Where'd they go?"

"They just vanished."

Red was focused on her hand, wondering how she did what she did. *I thought I didn't have my abilities. Did my anger overtake me again?* As she pondered, Bandit hopped back up to her shoulder and started licking her face again. Red laughed, "Now you cut that out!" Kyna and Kyani brushed themselves off and managed as best they could. Climbing back on into the carriage, the trio continued to the shore. Once they reached the edge of Korin, Red stared out into the waves for what seemed like forever. Cesna finally rose up onto the shore, as she did the first time she met Red.

"Legna? You've changed." She spoke, knowing the woman was the same one, by the way she'd been summoned.

"Thanks to Kyani here, I've regained my identity."

"You look, vaguely familiar," she continued, her head tilting left and right as the others just looked on confused, only hearing half of the conversation.

"You aren't the first one who has said that. I don't know why. But my true name is Red."

"Well let me guess, Red, you need another ride."

Red grinned. "I was hoping you could take us to…" she looked back at Kyani, "Where are we going again?"

Kyani's third eye flashed silver. "Kaatina."

"Isn't that were the other regency is?" pondered Kyna.

"Yeah, I believe so. I guess the other gates are there."

"How do we get there from here?" Red questioned, looking at Cesna.

"The easiest way is through Riverenda." The water bird huffed, *"Alright. Climb aboard."* The group climbed onto Cesna who, albeit reluctantly, started the long swim across the ocean towards Riverenda, as the suns set over the horizon.

⊰⊱⊰⊱⊰⊱⊰⊱⊰⊱⊰⊱⊰⊱⊰⊱⊰⊱⊰⊱⊰⊱

Alexander was sitting in his chair staring at the hole in the wall, letting the bright light burn his eyes. It was a new day now and the suns had just finished rising over Kaatina. Sitting there blankly, he let the shadow of his feelings consume his mind just as a figure came up behind him. She softly spoke, "Is there a reason you were hanging around that zavi?"

"Why is that any of your concern?" he asked sternly, slightly shifting his eyes to meet hers. "I could ask you the same thing."

She twirled a piece of red hair around her finger and remarked as if innocent, "I just wanted to know, I mean, you do know that we are one."

"Humph. Is that jealousy I hear in your voice? That never seemed to bother you before." he snorted, rolling his eyes, and flicking his hand in her direction, "Don't come to me acting like a wife now."

"Sweetie, don't get upset with me," she added, with mock hesitance. "You haven't been displaying the air of a rightful leader for some time now. You are putting your ancestors to shame, and disappearing in the face of adversity. The others are getting restless and using your name as an excuse to be defiant."

"And what does that have to do with me? They use any excuse to get what they want. That's always been the case." Alex shrugged, noting her swift change of subject.

"I don't know how long I can hold my dignity, being referred to as such a poor role-model's mate."

Alex stood at this, slamming his hands on the desk, while his brow furrowed. "Poor role-model's mate? Is that what you believe of me now?!" he urged, stepping towards her. "Or am I just not acting like your pawn as much as you expect? You must have noticed that I haven't been doing any more of your dirty work since Terrin was slain."

He could see Yeve flinch at this and knew he'd struck a nerve, "They just say that the leaders before you were much more efficient, stern and dependable."

"You didn't answer my question, *love*." He stared at his wife, a look of sheer annoyance on his face. He was tired of her wordplay, her tricks and most of all, her endless games.

Yeve simply rolled her eyes and turned, beginning to walk away. Stopping in mid-step, she raised a brow almost quizzically as she tilted her head back around and softly said, "Don't think I haven't noticed the many fights you've had with Zephyrus."

"OH! Did I hit a nerve?" Alexander hissed. He took a few steps up to her and looked her dead in the eyes, speaking now just as calmly as she had, his face just inches from hers. "Just because you feel the need to pretend to be a wife right now, doesn't mean I'm stupid enough to tell you my motives. Besides, you know as well as I do, whatever information you are trying so hard to get out of me you already know. So don't ask me any more stupid questions, or you'll find yourself needing a new place to live." He then pushed her aside and walked out of the room.

Yeve just smirked and watched him leave. "Oh my dear, someone will need a new place to live, but it surely won't be me, if I have anything to do about it…"

Blue eyes ducked and hid as the man stepped by. He smiled a bit as he watched Alex, until he disappeared around the corner. He checked to make sure the coast was clear, before slinking out of the corner and down the corridor, to the room where Alex exited from. Poking his head in the doorway, he saw Yeve's back to him, as she toyed with the missing piece of wall. As he stepped into the room, the sudden thud of his feet startled the woman and she turned immediately on her heels.

"What do you want?" she asked sternly, looking the man up and down quickly. Noting his yellow uniform, she pointed straight into his blue eyes. "Who are you? No one, who isn't a part of my regency, is allowed in the royal palace. Now get OUT!" she demanded and started to step towards him.

He jumped back and held up her hands. "Hey! One second, Your Highness. I am Ira, and I couldn't help but overhear your conversation." He bowed low hiding a snicker as he did.

"Your Highness?" The woman said raising a brow. "What *do* you want?" She grinned, "No one calls me that," she added, placing her hands upon her hips.

"I figured, since you are the mate of the leader that you deserve to be called with respect."

The red haired one laughed. "If I can help it, my respect will never be dependent upon my mate's actions, *nor* his rank." She paused, "Now tell me what it is you want, you really don't have to try and 'butter me up'."

"Do you have something *against* your mate?" he slyly grinned.

She chuckled, "I have a lot against my mate. What's that have to do with you?" There was a shrieking noise outside, as the man stepped closer.

"So why do you continue to put up with him?" he shrugged, "Surely you are more capable a leader, it should be no problem getting rid of him."

12 - Suicide Mission

"Sometimes those struggles, hardships and tough situations are there to stop you from going one way, and turning you around to where you need to be."
~Prime Sai Vasillico. <u>Reflections</u>

The group reached Riverenda the next evening and were utterly worn out. Cesna immediately camped out near the shore, curling into a huge ball and falling asleep almost instantly. The three looked around the landscape. Riverenda wore its name well, as the inita was nothing more than a cluster of smaller islands, connected by bridges. The islands were rocky grasslands, accented with many waterfalls. The trio began their trek into the village. They saw the hustle and bustle of an abundance of taira, the most populous species, in all of Zanali. While taira are the most diverse species they have no elemental or natural influence, so their villages relied on their intelligence and whatever technologies they'd been able to invent. The three came to the center of the village and gazed around at the huts and shops that were made in and around the waterfalls. It was then that Red got a strange sensation. "You ever get the feeling you were being watched?" she whispered to the others.

Kyna and Kyani, who still hadn't spoken more than a couple words to each other, looked around at her words. "I don't see anyone staring at us," responded Kyani.

"Well, you do still have that tiara on, and your third eye showing," chimed in Kyna. "If they stare at anything, it would be that."

Exodus II

"Why do you have to add your two cents into everything? Did anyone ask you?!" barked Kyani, balling her fists.

The two would have made a scene, if it weren't for Red shushing them, "Hey now… look over there," she whispered softly, motioning to the side of one of the shops. There, cowering between the buildings, was a little fennec fox, looking directly at them. Red smiled at the girl kneeling and holding out her hand.

"Now you know taira are taught not to come to strangers!" whispered Kyani.

Red smiled, "I'm not a stranger." She focused her mind on her natural element, love. She figured, if her anger could induce her old abilities, maybe love could too. As she focused on the girl, she did feel some of her old aura rising up within her and it warmed her from the inside out. The little fox tilted her head left and right but then slowly came out into the light, her ivory fur shining in the light of the suns. She wore a raspberry colored dress over a pale green puffed sleeved top and her beige hair was long and messy from the wind. She slowly and shyly sauntered over to Red, and looked up into the astrian's eyes. "Well, hello there, little one." The girl just smiled. "What's your name?"

"Me? Tiombe," she said softly, her tail wagging slowly.

"Tiombe Elodie!" an aqua and lavender haired woman yelled, as she hurried down the street. "How many times have I told you not to sneak off like that!"

"Rva!" the girl exclaimed and jumped into the woman's arms.

Rva turned her attention to the three. "Who are your friends, Ti?" Tiombe just shrugged. "You should know better than to talk to strangers!"

"Told you," whispered Kyani into Red's ear.

"I am Prima Sai Kyna." She bowed, as her sister chuckled.

"News flash, this isn't any of the lands of illura, no one knows you to be royalty, nor do they probably care."

Rva's eyes widened, "Did you say, illura?"

Kyani looked at her. "Yes ma'am. We are illura, my sister and I."

Red noticed Rva's eyes tear up a little. "I'm Rva." She held out her hand to them.

"My name is Kyani, this is my sister Kyna." She then acknowledged Red. "And this is Red."

The three shook hands before Rva smiled, her eyes still watery. "You…you must come and have supper with me, if you have the time."

"Actually, we were looking for some place to stay for the night," explained Red, noticing Tiombe reaching out to her from Rva's arms.

"Consider it done. Please follow me."

Taking the girl and giggling at her clinging, Red and the others followed Rva to a less populated area of Riverenda, near a tri colored waterfall. There was a medium sized hut, built inconspicuously near the waterfall. Here the group was given a room for the night, while Tiombe and Rva made them a nice supper. Red was inclined, or rather persuaded, to play with Tiombe, who'd warmed up to the angel.

When the group finally went to bed, it was another night Red was left awake. She was still thinking about her lost love and the pains that went with it. She also pondered on another thing. Why weren't any of the other angels here to help her? Were they all destroyed because of her? Was she really all alone? The more she dwelled on these things, the more she felt herself breaking. The only companion she had now was Bandit, who seemed to appear and disappear at will. Then again, she really didn't keep tabs on the little guy. Red sighed, turning in the bed, wondering if this journey would be worth anything if all her people were already destroyed, if she was already alone. Tears flowed down her face like rivers, and she cried until sleep finally washed over her:

Darkness as far as the eye could see. It moved with her, engulfed her, and filled every empty space. But it was a different darkness. This darkness wasn't cold. It didn't invoke fear. It wasn't intimidating or isolating. This darkness was friendly, warm, familiar. All too familiar. It felt like a protector, a father, keeping her enwrapped in its multiple layers. She couldn't see the light but she didn't need to. He saw it for her. All she had to do was relax and flow with the darkness. Red rose petals danced across the darkness like a soft wind, gently caressing her skin as they passed. Love. It was a love like she never knew, one that she'd thought she experienced previously, for so many years, but it was nothing compared to this love. This was genuine, long standing, unconditional love. She relaxed in the darkness' embrace and felt herself blossom. She could feel arms curl around her, the warmth igniting deep within her, rekindling a hope that had long since blown away. Then, the light she couldn't see before, suddenly poured through her bending and wrapping around the darkness but not completely destroying it. It grew from deep within her heart and outwards until the space where she laid in darkness' arms was filled with light. A light that could no longer be hidden.

"Sire!" came a shrill yell, as golden eyes widened in terror. Dymona jumped back, only to hear the resonating thud, as she bumped her head on the wall she leaned against. Rubbing her head, she pushed herself off the ground, "Why…?"

"This is where you decided to hide from my messengers?" he asked nonchalantly, his eyes coolly staring at her, between the fog covered floors. She looked up; even as she stood there, he towered above her. He was bent over slightly to compensate for the low ceilings of the catacomb.

"Hiding, Sire?" she squeaked, not wanting to admit her unusual choice of hangouts since Ambrose's imprisonment. She looked around for a moment trying to give the impression that she would never choose a dull place like this to hide.

The Sire gave a half smile. "Yes, hiding. You know very well that I have been sending messengers, to tell you important information, only to have them return and report that they could not find you. One of them caught you slipping through a door down this corridor and instead of trying to chase you, he came straight to me."

Dymona tilted her head upwards, to stare at him almost defiantly, "Who was the little snitch?!"

"Ahh, so it *is* true," he stated blatantly.

Dymona cringed. Slinking back to the ground and once again leaning against the wall, she folded her arms and gave a look of pure annoyance. "Fine…so I was hiding," she admitted under her breath.

The Sire gave a low chuckle. "I don't know why you turned rebellious on us all of a sudden, but that is neither here nor there. Right now I have important things to discuss with you." He turned his massive body around and sat on the floor to the side of her. The sound of his massive body hitting the floor resonated off the walls. Now he could straighten his back without knocking a hole in the ceiling. "My confidence in Noktuyn is wearing thin, and he has become obsessed with his current tasking. Because of this, I would rather not send him out on another errand. I've decided to assign the task to you. You are to track the Beast, getting close enough to see what it's doing. We need to know if it is actually benefitting our cause. If it isn't, we need to develop a plan to change that."

Dymona turned her eyes back to him and shook her head. "Don't you already have someone that is tracking it?" she stated quickly.

"Well, unfortunately, he is no longer with us," he countered, giving her a sly grin. "You see, he got a little too close and was no match for it."

"So, that's it, right? You are sending me on a suicide mission," she declared. "What if I don't want to do it? Huh? If you want me dead so bad, why don't you ju- waAAHH!" She immediately felt a sharp sting on her right arm where three fresh deep gashes throbbed, spanning from her shoulder to her elbow.

"I tolerated your hiding, but I will NOT tolerate your mouth!" the Sire roared, as he stood abruptly, blood dripping from his sharpened claws. "You have your orders, and I expect you to complete them. Understood, Le'Gless?" Dymona cringed. "The Beast's last whereabouts was somewhere near Nauti, Korin." The Sire only referred to others by their last name out of anger, which only heightened the hatred she already held against her last name. He lumbered a few steps, before glancing back at her. "You were once very high, but your mouth proved to be your biggest downfall. You may use that tone with Nagare if you wish, but not with me, else I may just take you up on that offer." He continued to storm off, carrying his large frame back down the catacomb and was out of sight moments later. Dymona sat, cowered in a ball carefully examining her wound. Her hand could only cover one of the three gashes made by the Sire's claws and the pain of it was searing, so much so that she didn't want to see what it looked like.

She scolded herself for her short temper. She removed her hand from the wounded arm and placed it on the wall. Green liquid made an imprint of her hand on the wall, as she used it as a brace in order to pick herself up.

I love the way he gives me a task, after wounding something as vital as my arm.

Standing now, she reflected someone whose arm was broken and not just severely gashed, as she turned her gaze to peer down the hall. She turned the opposite way and slowly went down the hall to the door that the snitch had caught her going through. Dymona took a deep breath, before making her way to her room. Passing zavi stared at her, some with disgust and others with shock. She ignored them both. Once inside her room, she let the gravity of what The Sire said, fully run through her mind. He was trying to get rid of her, but she didn't know why. Now that she really thought about it, she didn't even know why the Council felt Ambrose was a threat. Dymona wondered if trying to break him out made her just as much of a threat as Ambrose was. The logic didn't add up. Sure he somehow made other zavi fear him, mostly ones from other clans that didn't work with him on a daily basis, but to her he'd never shown any indication of having an advantage to anyone, especially the Council. All Dymona knew was that he hated the Council with a passion, but, at the same time, became obsessed with becoming a part of it. Well, that logic didn't make sense either. There were definitely pieces of this situation that she didn't know, and that Ambrose was surprisingly good at hiding. Now if only she could stay alive long enough to find out what those missing pieces were. Dymona settled on the fact she would have to find

Exodus II

where the Beast was at least, but she refused to be like the former tracker. Though the Sire wanted her to get close to it, she wasn't about to. She would get just enough information to keep him off her back, until she could really free Ambrose and figure out what all this is really about.

"What really lurks in the night? Are you sure there isn't anything there when you turn out the lights?" ~Kotovo. <u>Escaping the Night</u>

Kyani's third eye woke her early the next morning, as if it were anxious about something. She groggily moved barely opening her eyes and mumbling under her breath, "That blessing is starting to be more trouble than its worth." She yawned and looked around the room, but nothing looked out of place. "Ugh, what is wrong with you?" she asked at the eye. It was then that whispers came from the other room,

"What the heck were you thinking?"

"Will you keep it down?! You will wake them all up."

"No one is supposed to know this exists!"

"Lay off. What did you expect me to do, leave them out there to sleep? They aren't from around here anyway and it's not like I took them straight to the library."

"Still, you better watch it."

Kyani heard some footsteps and yawned, really too sleepy to try to figure out what the conversation was about. Her eye was still burning, alert. She wondered if it meant that another gate was nearby.

As the others woke, Rva walked in the room, turning the light on, which got rousing yells of agony. "Morning all! I brought you breakfast!" She sat a large tray on the table, at the far side of the room. Tiombe followed behind her, carrying a stack of cups and a large pitcher of juice. The group yawned, stretched and finally joined the two at the table, while Rva divvied the juice between the cups. After Red led them in prayer, they enjoyed the breakfast.

"Thank you for all of this." Red nodded, smiling at Rva.

"It's my pleasure."

Kyani looked at her. "Which reminds me, why were you so eager to offer us such hospitality?"

Rva paused, smiling softly. "A favor to an old friend."

"That is why you were holding back tears?" questioned Red, remembering how much her eyes were watering.

Rva nodded. "He was an illura, and the only man I ever fell in love with."

Kyna's ears perked up, "What's his name? Maybe we know him."

"His name was-" her words were cut off by the sound of people yelling and scrambling outside, like an evacuation.

"What is all the commotion?" Kyani asked, as they all rushed to the window. Seeing the chaos, they went outside only to find three yaitali causing a big disturbance in the waters. Two of them were trying to hold back the third from charging onto the land. The yaitali that was struggling desperately to get to shore was a deep orange, with the normal black underbelly. Its tails were amber and gold. Finally he broke free of the other yaitali and made it to shore just as the group met them there. When Kyani saw the yaitali her eye started throbbing and she doubled over holding her head.

"Are you OK?" Red asked, catching the illura and trying to hold her up.

"I don't know, it's...it's my eye."

Red raised a brow. "Are you trying to hold it back?"

"I don't know, maybe. I don't know what it will do."

"Just let it be free." Kyani looked at Red hesitantly. "Let The Exalted One work how He wants to work through you," consoled Red, lifting Kyani's chin.

Kyani smiled, standing up and taking a deep breath, relaxing and trying to clear her mind. The eye opened and like a rush of water the beam of light came forth and this time engulfed the amber yaitali. Red and Kyna looked at each other confused until the light cleared. Where the yaitali once stood, lay a man. Seeing the man, Rva rushed over and lifted him up, to lean on her.

"Xurian," she whispered, hardly believing her eyes. Red stared, the name being very familiar to her. Then the memory played in her head of a man dying by the hands of Ira. This crying woman laid over his body and a pardon by The Exalted One saying that it wasn't his time yet. Now she knew why.

Xurian coughed a few times and slowly opened his eyes, looking straight up into Rva's and he smiled, "Thank ye, miss."

It was like nails piercing her heart. He really didn't remember her, just like the angel had said. "Y… you can just call me Rva." She spoke softly to him, "And just relax until you get your strength."

Eva ran in wondering what the commotion was and stopped short seeing the man she'd caused the death of, alive and well. "What happened here?"

Rva looked up at her. "Meet Xurian. Xurian, this is my sister Eva."

The man turned his eyes to the other lady and gave a weak nod. "M'Pleasure."

Exodus II

Eva was transfixed and confused, wondering why she was acting like he didn't remember them. Didn't remember what happened. "Sure I know Xurian. Don't I?"

Rva glared. "Don't mind her." She looked at Kyna, "Would you help me get him inside?" Kyna nodded and the two shuffled him into the house and got him laid on the couch. Rva then pulled Eva into the kitchen by her ear. The group could hear rebuking whispers for a while, but couldn't make out what was being said. After a few moments Rva poked her head back in. "We will fix some soup. Keep an eye on him, k?"

Eva came out about a half hour later with the soup but didn't say much as she doled it out to the group. She also kept glancing at Xurian uncomfortably. Kyani looked from Kyna to Xurian wondering how she would find the last gate. This was the time that Red really wished she had her full powers and abilities, there could be so much she could do to ease the circumstances. The rest of the day was spent helping Xurian regain his strength and explaining what had happened. Xurian agreed to help the cause as a thanks for restoring his true form, and the group set out to find the fourth gate in Esailles the following day.

⤜⤐⤜⤐⤜⤐⤜⤐⤜⤐⤜⤐⤜⤐⤜⤐⤜⤐⤜⤐⤜⤐⤜⤐

Alex was outside, gazing up at the sky, trying to calm his nerves. The moons were shining brightly and the sight was enough to put a small smile on his face. "What's this…" he whispered suddenly as he gazed around his atmosphere. The man's deep yellow-green eyes were focused and cool, chilling out from the side of one of the buildings, hidden in the darkness of the corner. He stood stock still, with a half-bemused look on his face thinking he was sneaking up on the illura.

"Zephyrus…" Alex whispered to himself. "Why is he here?" he asked himself, with a furrowed brow and uneasy twitch of his tail. Zephyrus moved his body close to the ground and allowed the white of his fangs to show in the moonlight. And then it made sense. "I see you, you know. You are insulting me, thinking I don't see you." Zephyrus didn't bother answering, just leaped at Alex, charging energy to the end of his tail and wrapping it around Alex's neck. Surges of electricity flowed through the tip of his tail sending volts through Alex's body. Then Zephyrus let go, watching him tumble to the ground. Alex hunched over, trying painfully to pick himself back up. "I am finally going to get rid of you for good. Once that serenda woman is dead and the beast comes to rule, our species will overtake your band of dark knights. Then we will show you what a *true* assassin is." Alex's eyes narrowed and his body vanished into the ground. From the cover of the shadows, he watched Zephyrus's anger bubble over. "Come out of hiding, you coward!" he scowled, running to the spot where Alex's body was supposed to be. Through the shadows, Alex reached up, grabbing Zephyrus's legs, causing him to fall forward. The shadow walker then appeared behind him, but before he could get a grip on the fallen zavi, Zephyrus lashed out his tail, slicing his arm. The zavi pulled himself from the ground, wiping the blood away from his lips. Alex went to disappear into the shadows again but Zephyrus quickly wrapped his tail around the illura's neck, before he could fully disappear. "Oh no you don't." He pulsed electricity through Alex's body, watching the man squirm in pain. Zephyrus reveled in it a while before tossing him into the side of the building. This time, Alex tried to stand again but failed, realizing how much the shocks had weakened him. By now, Zephyrus was standing over him, and started shocking him in short spurts just for the added fun of seeing his body jump with each one.

Out of nowhere, a fist made contact with the back of Zephyrus's head and he fell to the side. He rolled around to see Dymona standing there. "Peekaboo."

Exodus II

"Really, Dymona?" Zephyrus rubbed the back of his head. "Really, that much of a traitor huh?" His body rose back to a standing position.

"Rather a traitor than a two-faced backstabber," she responded, bracing herself for his reaction. He roared, shooting a ball of electricity at her. She ducked and rolled out of the way. "Try again." He whipped his tail at her, but she grabbed it instead, holding the tip away from her and tugging on it. Zephyrus crashed back to the ground. While he was picking himself back up, she ran over to Alex. Pulling him to his feet, she braced him against the wall. "Are you alright?" she asked not realizing her opponent's recovery. Alex pushed his weight onto her and shielded her from the electric blast that erupted on the wall above them. "Oh this is ridiculous," Dymona said, pushing Alex back against a non-scorched part of the wall and getting back on her own feet. Glaring at Zephyrus, she took a few steps towards him, and away from Alex, almost like she was circling him. "Come on, try and hit me." Zephyrus grinned sending a barrage of electricity at her, but with her agility she gracefully dodged everyone. Rolling, ducking, and flipping, Dymona stayed on top of everything he shot at her. She noticed the beams getting thinner and thinner until he ran out of his internal power. Now it was Dymona who was grinning. "I've learned a thing or two about our mannerisms. Bred to go for any chance we get without thinking of the consequences," she explained, calmly making her way closer to him. "How do you think I orchestrated the Great Death?" Zephyrus growled again, lunging at her, but she jerked his arm away and punched him square in the face. "Once we reach a point of madness, we are useless without being Ultima. We are irrational, like animals, following only instinct instead of logic," she added, grabbing his arm and swinging his body into the wall. This time he fell, and found he didn't have the strength to lift himself up again.

Coughing up blood, he slid his body up to a standing position, glared at Dymona. "Don't worry, you are going to end up just like that dolt, Ambrose," then turned on his heels, leaving the area.

14- Visions and Vendettas

"Is it me or are we still worlds apart? Or could it be…that I see beyond the very things that blind you…" ~Prime Sai Vasillico. <u>Reflections</u>

"I think Zephyrus has become obsessed." Said Dymona long after he'd gone. "He's had a vendetta against that serenda girl and now has taken to trying to kill you."

Alex laughed, holding his side. "Glad I'm that important to someone." He led her out to the shore, kneeling to dip his hands into the water, to partake of the cool liquid. "So what did he mean by the 'you will end up just like Ambrose' bit?" He could feel some of his strength returning.

She narrowed her eyes. "Apparently, our council has deemed a fellow zavi a threat, for some unknown reason, and locked him away in the dungeons." She folded her arms. "Since he was really the only person I've ever confided in, I felt obligated to try and break him out," she continued, trying to make it sound as if there were no weird feelings surrounding her intentions. "Now I've been made just as much a target as he has and been sent on a mission they are hoping I don't come back from alive."

Alex sipped more of the ocean water from his hands. "I thought you were already a traitor."

"I am. But they left me alone until I tried to break him free." She sighed. "Whatever it is he found out, The Council is really trying to keep it from being exposed."

Alex thought about this for a while, as he kneeled there, staring far out across the ocean. He thought about his current situation, as well as Dymona's. He thought about his wife, and how tired he was of being her doormat. He wanted to be free. He wanted to be himself. He no longer wanted to be defined by his ancestors. He felt strange; as his eyes scanned the horizon, he felt a silent urge, like a small, still voice, that wanted him to help her. He weighed his options, but the still voice touched his heart and a warmth filled his body. He wasn't sure if it was The Exalted One or not, but decided to take a chance. He turned to Dymona and grinned. "How about we really stir things up then?"

"What do you mean?" Dymona raised a brow suspiciously.

Alex disappeared into the shadows and then reappeared right behind Dymona, whispering in her ear "Let's break him out."

Dymona screamed, jumping away from him and staring, "What are you doing?! Are you crazy?!"

Alex laughed more. "Crazy? Yes." He showed his fangs, "Always have been." He took a few steps closer to her, "Let's be crazy together. What have you got to lose?"

Dymona still looked at him suspiciously. "Why do you want to help me all of a sudden?" Her hands hugged her hips. "Besides, you are in no condition to do anything."

Alex shrugged with a maniacal grin. "Didn't you say one becomes irrational once madness sets in?"

She pointed at him. "That's only for zavi. Anger and rage tend to do that."

"As a sentinel, we are taught not to let the wounds of the body prevent us from doing what needs to be done." He glanced at her.

"What about the wounds in your brain?!" she flailed. "What do you really want?"

"Nothing," he chuckled, "That paranoid, huh?" he smirked. "What if I said I just wanted to help you?"

"I'd say you were lying."

"Then are you lying about your motives for trying to break him out?" he mused, taking a step closer.

"What does one thing have to do with the other?" she countered, stepping back.

"If you are so bent against anything but hate, you wouldn't have *cared* enough to try and get him out. You'd be just like Zephyrus. But you aren't."

"So?" she asked, incredulously.

"So, why can't I *care* enough to help you, even if it's not a normal reflection of my past?"

"People don't change like that."

"You did."

"You don't even know me."

"So you're saying your past still defines you?" Alex quipped, quirking his brow.

Dymona opened her mouth, but realized he had a point. She narrowed her eyes, "No-one helps me."

"Does that mean no one should?"

He had another point. Her fists clenched in frustration, "FINE. You win." She held her head. "My head hurts now."

Alex chuckled again. "Stop trying to analyze it so much." He smiled. "You aren't the evil person you want others to think you are. You also aren't someone that doesn't deserve a bit of kindness."

Exodus II

She was still holding her head. "I just don't understand you."

"Who says you are supposed to?"

"Because you seem to know a lot about me, to say you don't know me."

"No wonder your head hurts." He chuckled. "Just allow me to help you, alright?"

Dymona growled in sheer frustration, "FINE."

He smiled. "Great, we should start heading back to Zavare." He ushered her towards the ocean. "We will break him out tonight."

In front of the Esailles Palace, a massive crowd formed, like many ants culminating out of their home. The sun cascaded rays of light that glistened off of the palace walls. Between the two tall towers there stood a woman about 5'4" with short red hair, sun touched like flames sweeping over her left eye and grazing the edge of her neck. She had deep money green eyes, cold yet bold against her pale beige skin. She wore a long black trench coat whose ends gracefully grazed the ground beneath her. A silky maroon dress was worn underneath. It was made of crushed velvet and was low cut, utterly low. Maroon gloves slid over her hands and arms accented with a pearl bracelet that matched the triple pearl earrings that hid underneath the flaming wisps of hair near her ears. On her feet were long, black boots, with six inch heels that cast a deep resonating sound when she walked. The coat moved swiftly in the wind of the afternoon with the ends of the dress, as the trees waved at her from high above. She stood on a tree stump that was brought by two of her sentinels. In the audience were all the many illura that held her in high interest and esteem. Also in the mix were Red, Xurian, Kyani and Kyna, who'd just found their way into the regency that day and were curious about the gathering. A slight smile crept upon her face as she slowly looked at the masses eager to continue a plan she'd carefully constructed. With one raised hand the crowd silenced and she could see all eyes upon her.

"My people. Fair people of Kaatina. The beautiful Esailles Regency. Hear me, as I speak to you." A slight pause, simply for dramatics, something she well excelled at. "As you know, our regency has established a long and solid agreement with the zavi. It is because we are working together, that we have a strong standing power within our community. Am I right?" The crowd cheered. " This caused the crowd to begin a discussion and she raised her voice to speak above them. "I've gathered you here, in order to inform you that *your* Prime Sai has repeatedly fought with the very zavi we have utilized to help our cause! As your Prima Sai, I sit back and witness the ties to our strength, our power, and our dominate leadership, become unraveled at his hands! Is this what we accept as our role model? Are we to just stand here and tolerate it?! What if the zavi launched a full out attack on our regency, simply over your Prime Sai's selfish decisions?! Do we have to suffer for his pitiful leadership?" Her followers began to get rowdy.

A man, standing three rows from her, thought a moment and then raised a hand up, taking icy blue strands from his face, and spoke hesitantly, "But Prima Sai, he did go through with the execution of Terrin."

"That wasn't a mission, just simply a show of power and *not* the topic in question," she said sternly, eyes narrowing to fix upon him with a stare so intense, it caused him to shudder and take a step back into the crowd. Kyani searched the crowd for the one who asked the question and she grabbed Kyna's sleeve in earnest.

Exodus II

"What is it?" groaned Kyna, not at all interested in whatever her sister was going through.

"B…blue hair…from dark…to white…a full array of love…he will show me one night…" Kyna knew the phrase, it was one her sister had recited so many times, a prophecy she'd received that neither one thought would ever come true. Kyna looked at the man and she'd never before seen one that had that kind of hair, and she never thought she ever would either. At the same time Kyani's third eye throbbed, the same way it had before and she knew they'd found the last gate. "The *question* is," Yeve demanded, causing the sisters to come back to the situation at hand, "how long are we going to let him continue as the Prime Sai while setting the type of example we would have never allowed in the past?" she searched the faces of all those that watched her, for just one who would dare speak up and even more so, try and argue against her. Then, that same one, with ice blue hair, paused a moment and spoke again.

"So…what exactly are you saying, Prima Sai?" he asked, still keeping a low profile among the crowd, strategically standing among those much taller than him.

Yeve turned her eyes again to him, but this time she smiled, "We exile him," she said dryly, but with a touch of anxiousness. The guy's eyes widened in surprise and he exclaimed,

"Have you gone MAD, woman? No one in history has EVER exiled a lord before!" He looked around frantically for someone to help him out, but no one spoke, instead they all gave him the look of a traitor. He quickly changed his thinking, and, after swallowing a mighty gulp of his terror, said, "B-besides, none of us have the power enough to exile him. The only one with power over him is… *The Exalted One.*"

Yeve's brow raised, as the mass of people started to chatter among themselves. "The Exalted One may have, but so do I." She smiled wickedly.

The man turned his back to her. "You *can't* be serious. No one would be idiotic enough to try and compare themselves to the Exalted One!"

Yeve simply lowered her voice an octave and stooped low to the crowd. "No-one is doing that. I'm simply saying majority rules and, as his mate, I *am* the one who can give the final say to him."

"…Mate? More like overbearing mother…" he muttered under his breath. The guys standing around him chuckled a bit at his retort. The laughter caused her to straighten up and narrow her eyes. Then, in a voice that pierced the air, shocking the crowd into a frozen state, she proclaimed,

"I am his second in command and by that right I can overpower his rule, if the majority is with me. He will be exiled at the end of the week." Then she peered down at the man again "And I assure you, I have the majority at my disposal." Yeve turned and closely scanned the crowd again. "If any of you disagree with me, you better make sure your mind is changed by that time. Else you won't like me afterwards and the feeling will be mutual." She smirked, before gazing triumphantly over their heads. The words sent uneasy chills down his body, as his mind tried to frantically think of something else to say. The masses cheered her on again, forgetting the points he made only a moment before.

"Don't you think The Exalted One will backlash at you for trying to do something only He has done?!" he yelled, more loudly than he had expected beforehand but, with a sheer look of terror and pleading in his facial features.

She turned to look at him, annoyed even more fully now. "If you don't want to be a part of my plan, then I suggest you leave.

Exodus II

You are trying my patience and, if you continue with your sense-less babble, I will have to silence you myself." She then reached and caught hold of the hilt of her dagger that hung underneath her cloak. Seeing this he swallowed again and turned his back to her, making his way through the crowd. Taking a deep breath as he walked, he wondered how Alexander would pull himself out of this one. As he maneuvered his way through the crowd, he was met by three friendly faces.

"It was very admirable of you to stand your ground back there." Kyani complimented softly, so as not to startle him, as they joined him, walking further away from the masses.

Stevan looked up to see the three unfamiliar ladies and bowed. "Thank you kindly, though I don't think it did any good."

"Sometimes things may not go the way you want them to with your eyes…" voiced Red, "but you never know who is watching you, or how your decisions affect people you've never met."

Kyani gave Red a weird look, before commenting, "What she means is, it's important that you stood your ground, no matter the outcome."

Stevan chuckled a bit. "I've never seen you around here before, are you new?" he asked, noting the colors of their dress didn't match the colors of Esailles or Terralyn.

"My sister, Kyani, and I are from Metayale," Kyna answered.

"Oh? I am Stevan Sivyr. What brings you here?"

"Ms. Astrian here." Kyani giggled, as Stevan looked at Red in disbelief.

"Oh yeah, right, who are you really?" he quipped dismissing the claim.

Red struck a pose, as her angel wings gracefully appeared behind her and, with a wink, politely responded, "You tell me."

"Nooooo!" Stevan gasped. "For real? Like you're a for real angel?"

"As opposed to a what?" jested Xurian, waving his arms as if he had wings. "A for fake one?"

Stevan folded his arms. "Oh, very funny. You know what I meant." He gaped at Red again. "What in the world would an angel want here?"

"You, Of course," Red stated, opening her hand out to him.

He just stared down at her open palm. "Me?"

"I've gotten to see this routine twice already," giggled Kyani more.

"Oh, be quiet!" her sister scolded, putting her hand over Kyani's mouth.

"I need your help," she explained. "My home has been lost in the chaos and you are the fourth gate I need, to help me restore it."

Stevan croaked, "But how do you know it's me that you need…" His words were stopped as Kyani's third eye awakened and showered Stevan in the same blinding, white light. Afterwards, he matched Xurian and Kyna in embroidered clothing, only his right arm was left bare, where his illura symbol shone, just the opposite of Xurian.

"That tells you," Kyani nodded, feeling oddly proud of herself, even if she really didn't have control of her third eye.

"A Seer?!" questioned Stevan, wondering how he missed the full third eye before. He was on the verge of a mental breakdown, trying to piece it all together.

Exodus II

"Calm down, ye," smiled Xurian. "It's a big shock to us all."

"But we are in this together," cheered Kyani. "Who wouldn't want to help out an Astrian?"

"And actually see what it means to be the gates," continued Kyna.

Stevan took a deep breath, wondering if everything he dismissed as a myth, was true and for a moment he remembered Eshe and all the silly things she believed. Maybe they weren't so silly after all. He thought of the surprised look she would have, when he told her this. "Ok. I'm in. On one condition." He smiled at Red. "I'd like you to meet my sister, because it would mean the world to her."

Red thought on this for a moment but eventually smiled back. "It's a deal."

Figure 7 - Ambrose T'Nagare

15- Betraya

"People say a lot of things about love, but I have learned one thing. Love is nothing without hope. Love can bring fear and hurt, but only hope can overcome it. Through hope, we are able to find true love and only from love can we be at peace with one another." ~ Dymona. <u>From Heaven to Home</u>

Once night fell and stilled, Alex and Dymona made their way through Zavare. Dymona took the lead, showing Alex the secret passages around and above the caves where the zavi were either sleeping, or getting ready to hunt. Most were already gone, leaving empty caves. They took their time in the catacombs waiting for as many zavi to leave for the hunt as possible.

"Do you even know how we are going to do this?" Dymona asked, climbing up onto a protruding rock, to cross over a deep valley.

"That is none of your concern. You let me handle it."

Dymona's feet hit the rock and she stopped, turning to him. "How can I not be concerned? I just went through this a few nights ago."

Alex landed near her and smiled. "For once, just once, can't you trust a man to guide you?"

Dymona roared, "I am a strong zavi woman, who is quite capable of taking care of herself!"

He sighed, "It's not about that, Dymona," he began, taking her hand. "I know you are fully capable and independent. But it is my honor and duty to be able to help protect you."

Exodus II

She sneered, as she snatched her hand away, "No one would be so foolish. I don't need your protection."

"Foolish?" he mused, tilting his head a bit. "I honestly can't understand why someone so proud, would demean herself in such a way." He shrugged, passing her, as they continued on.

"What's that supposed to mean?!" she yelled, running to catch up to him.

Alex halted, so suddenly that she almost ran into the back of him. "That you would see yourself as unworthy of someone wanting to treat you as such." He waited a moment, but didn't turn around. He knew that her silence meant he'd struck a nerve. He continued walking. "So here's the deal. You just act like you are going to visit Ambrose, and let me handle the rest."

"I don't..."

"And if you come into any danger at all, I will never ask you to trust me again."

"Fine," she muttered, not wanting to admit he had a point. The two exited the catacombs, right before getting to the dungeons. When she finally crossed into the first main dungeon, she noticed that Alex was nowhere to be found. She was about to call him every name in the book for leaving her, when she heard a whisper near her ear.

"I'm still here. Go on."

Creepy was the first thought that came to her, but she pushed the feeling to the back of her mind. She was making her way towards Ambrose's cell, when two guards met her. *Here we go again*, she thought, watching the two study her. It seemed like the only cell that was heavily guarded tonight, was his. Picked by the Sire himself, she gathered, noticing how the two were larger and more muscular than the normal guards.

"Looks like we are going to have some fun tonight." One started with a sly grin.

"Yeah, we are gonna have ta search ya sweetie," said the other, running a finger along her shoulder, and eager to put his hands on her. Just as he edged closer to her, a voice resonated in his ears,

"It isn't polite to touch a lady without permission."

"What tha-?!" the guard shrieked looking for the source. A hand reached out from his own shadow on the wall beside him and grabbed his neck, shoving him violently into the other guard. The only sound was the clash of their heads colliding and their bodies hitting the ground. Dymona stared at the still bodies. In all the time she spent around the illura, she never saw one do anything vaguely close to what she just witnessed.

"How did you do that?"

She heard Alex chuckle, "Just call it a gift."

The noise was enough to stir Ambrose, who'd been failing at his attempts to sleep. "Dymona? Is that you?"

"Pike down, idiot," she scolded, reaching the bars of his cell, "I've come to get you out."

"Again?!" he yelled in whisper.

"Don't be funny." She pointed behind him, "This time I brought help."

Ambrose turned to see the shadows merge and become solid. "Holy crap! What is that?"

"I have a name you know." Alex stated, fully formed now.

"Will you keep it down?!"

Exodus II

"Where there is darkness and shadows there I am." Alex grinned mischievously.

"You sound like a superhero reject," Dymona added, turning to see four more guards closing in on them, having heard all the commotion. "Told you to keep your big mouth shut."

"No sweat," Alex smirked, "This is the fun part." He vanished into the shadows on the far wall of the cell.

"What's going on here?!" the tallest of the four growled.

"Why are you here?" glared another, grabbing Dymona's arm.

"I don't know why you insist on manhandling beautiful women." Alex's voice echoed, making all four guards freeze. *Beautiful?* Both Dymona and Ambrose thought, exchanging puzzled glances. They watched as the fog rose around the zavi guards, pulling the shadows from every corner of the room. The guards, alert now, moved nervously through the mist, their eyes blinded in the dark haze. Then to their amazement, the shadows moved around the guards, and one by one, knocked each of the guards to the ground. It looked like they were wrestling and fighting directly with a myriad of shadows. They lost, and four cold bodies lay still on the dungeon floor.

Alex appeared again and moved the fog up around the bars of Ambrose's cell. "Now let's get him out." Ambrose looked on with disbelief, thinking that, while Alex could manipulate shadows in order to fight, there was no way he could break through the cell bars. Alex noticed his expression and mused, "Ye of little faith." He grinned slyly, as the fog gathered around all the bars, casting a 3D shadow of the bars perpendicular to the cell. It was then the two zavi witnessed the true divine power behind the illura's gift. As they examined the shadow more closely, they realized the shadow cast by the fog had actually moved the bars, leaving a large hole in its wake. Dymona entered the cell and put Ambrose's arm around her shoulders, helping him stumble through the hole. Once they were clear of the cell, Alex dispersed the fog, releasing the shadow cast from it and leaving the cell appearing untouched. The two stared in awe for a moment, before Alex urged them to leave.

"But where are we going to go?" asked Dymona, knowing that once the two made it out of Zavare, they could never come back.

Ambrose wheezed a bit, trying to get his voice. "We should go to Eagali," he suggested. "It will be the safest place for us."

"That will be the first place the zavi will search!" yelled Dymona, thinking Ambrose daft for even suggesting it.

He sighed. "Then let them find me." His eyes weakly looked up at her. "Other than our home, it is the only place I am familiar with." He coughed, breathing more heavily, "I am in no condition to go someplace new, it's not like we are welcomed with open arms, you know."

Dymona hesitated at first, but finally relented. "As you wish." She placed his arm back around her and started helping him towards the northeastern shore. As the two passed Alex, he stopped, "Thank you." He said softly, holding out his hand.

Alex smiled, shook his hand and nodded. "No problem. Though you really should be thanking the lady here, for allowing me to help her cause."

For the first time in her life, Dymona blushed and couldn't even respond. Ambrose looked over at her and smiled more, the two men noticing the bright blue of her cheeks. "Thank you as well," his eyes stared deep into hers, "for everything you've shown me."

Exodus II

Dymona looked puzzled. "Shown you?"

He nodded. "You know exactly what you've shown me." He glanced at Alex, then back at her. "The same things you are being shown."

Figure 8 - Dragon Tower

16- The Gate

❧❧❧❧❧❧❧❧❧❧❧❧❧❧❧❧❧❧❧❧❧❧

"Well, now that all of us are together, what are we supposed to do?" shrugged Kyani, as the group stood just outside the gates of Esailles, waiting for something dramatic to happen.

"Would this be what the gate tower is for?" asked Xurian, remembering the tower being a mandatory addition to every regency, though no one ever recalled them being used.

Kyna tilted her head at him, "Is that what those things are for?" She grinned. "Well, the title fits."

"So where is the Esailles Gate Tower located?" asked Kyani looking around.

Stevan smiled. "Not too far from here." He smiled at Kyani, "Allow me to lead."

Kyna glanced at Kyani, with a small smile as the group moved across the land, towards a tall tower sitting in the distance. Its windows and door were topped with crescent moons, while its top was a cluster of four, red teardrop shaped tips. The tower was made of a deep blue bricks, which only made the golden stones that held the tower tips in place, glow even brighter. As the others stepped inside, they were surprised that the inside looked so much bigger than it did from the outside. Stevan and Kyna went around the base of the tower lighting the torches so they could see. Once all the torches were lit, the five saw a bright flash of light, and a star appeared, twinkling right in front of Red. When the flash dimmed, a large gleaming gold coin appeared rotating in midair.

Exodus II

When Red grasped it, the face of the coin changed. Like a small video snippets of Alex's rescue of Ambrose played for the group.

"What do you suppose it means?" pondered Kyna.

"Means the Prime Sai is going to have even more trouble when he gets back," sighed Stevan.

"This looks like one of the coins on the slate." Red examined it, looking at the coin more closely. When the flashbacks stopped, the coin reduced itself in size, to fit neatly in her palm, its face carrying an unfamiliar symbol. "No time to figure it out now, we have more important things to figure out." Red placed the coin in her pocket, before surveying the room again. Glancing down, she noticed some writing in the center of floor, scrawled inside a large crescent moon.

When two or more are gathered, I am in the midst.

The miracle you are seeking will happen from such as simple as this.

Red pondered it a moment, after reading it aloud. "Well…let's gather together."

The group formed a circle, holding hands, and for a while nothing happened. But as they closed their eyes, focusing their thoughts on the Exalted One, they started to hear a rumble in the room. Opening their eyes, they noticed a glow emanating off of each of them: Kyani in white, Kyna in cyan, Xurian in magenta and Stevan in yellow. As they glowed, the illura symbols on their skin grew warm and projected its image high above their heads. The symbols, were ancient Asta, the language of the Astrians and when the four were put together a single word emerged:

REDEMPTION

At this, the tower trembled and shook, causing the group to look up, viewing the four tower tips split away from each other and letting the night sky pour in. They felt a downdraft of wind that carried in the stars from the sky as if the night sky itself moved to fill the tower. Out of the star trail a great dragon formed, moving through darkness itself. Its silver tipped fur twinkled like the stars and his eyes had flecks of every color imaginable. He curled around the outside of the tower, his sheer body mass too large to fit inside. His wings were made out of the dark sky and were sprinkled with stars. The same winged symbols found on Red's shoulders appeared on his, only his were rainbow in hue and were blazing reflections off of his black fur. His iridescent eyes caught sight of Red and as their eyes locked she felt a familiar warm feeling that delved deep into her heart.

"You seem so familiar." She spoke, moving towards the area where his head was, and feeling surrounded by the dragon's aura.

The dragon just smiled. "Well, I've always been with you." He folded his massive wings on his back. "You may not have always seen me, and I wasn't always able to speak, but you have never been alone." Silent tears formed in Red's eyes, as she stared into his. "Nor will you ever be alone, as long as I live."

"But who -"

The dragon shook his head. "That's not important right now. The important thing is fulfilling what you all have called me to do." The dragon raised its neck back and the huge rainbow colored chain necklace caught the light of the torches. Its center charm was a black and greyscale ring, surrounding a red heart with a black cross in it. The charm faced Red and glowed hot and Red felt the heat rise up within her and she glowed.

"My powers!" she exclaimed.

"Yes." The dragon nodded as the charm's glow dimmed. But with the restoration of her powers, came the renewing of her broken memories. The vision of the destruction of the Spectrums played over and over in her head and the heaviness of guilt bared on her shoulders. She was the one who caused it all. That's why no one was there to help her, she didn't even know what happened to all her people. Fearing the worst she looked back up at the dragon but before she could ask her dreaded question he put a finger to his lips before continuing, "Now for the main thing." He uncurled himself from around the tower, and flew back into the sky. Spinning in the air, the dragon made the darkness warp and twist before their eyes. Constellations parted and regrouped with different combinations of stars. Then the darkness broke, causing them to see something normally impossible to view with the naked eye. The group felt the ground shake as the edges of one of the spectrums opened through the stars. The watched in awe as pieces of the adjoining spectrums rebuilt themselves, sending reflections of its light through the darkness.

"What is that?" asked Stevan.

"It's... part of Astria, The Spectrums, where we live," she said, overjoyed at seeing it. "So it wasn't destroyed?"

"Yes, Milady, It was." The dragon bellowed from the sky, "But the gates have come together to allow me to restore it."

"Redemption..." Red said, low to herself, realizing something as she gazed up again, "So this journey The Exalted One led me on, the wooden tablet, finding the gates...it became atonement for my wrath?"

The dragon nodded, "True redemption was the only power that could be the catalyst for the Spectrums rebirth."

"The Spectrums?" Stevan gaped. "You mean, it really exists?"

"I exist, don't I?" Red tilted her head at Stevan.

"Oh, yeah…sorry."

"You cannot get there though," added the dragon before Red could get too excited.

"Why?" Her heart sank.

"You must finish what you started long ago. Once you've defeated all whom you seek, you will be able to reach home once again." The dragon then vanished into the darkness and the sky returned to normal.

"But h -" Red started, lifting her hand towards the sky, as the dragon disappeared. "Don't leave me…" she whispered softly, her head falling in sorrow.

The four walked up to her, Kyani putting her hand on Red's shoulder. "Aww, don't be sad," she whispered. "You'll get back home." Red gave them a weak smile, as they slowly headed out of the tower. As they left the tower, another small form poked its head out from the crack in the door. It watched the group a moment before scampering quickly off in the opposite direction, its coat blending in with the night.

Xurian grinned and stretched, "We unleashed some kind of dragon! Can you believe it? That dragon was cool looking!"

"Well… yeah, but that's really all we did…" Kyani muttered wondering if all the trouble was worth it.

"You actually restored the Spectrums beyond the clouds." Chimed Red, still sorrowful that she couldn't return home. "And that is nothing to be taken lightly."

Red looked over at them and shook off her emotions. "I should start heading to Eagali," she said to the group. "There I can start searching for the beast." She bowed to the gates. "Thank you for coming and helping me."

Exodus II

Kyna exclaimed, "What are you talking about? We aren't going to let you fight something alone!"

"Don't you need to go back and be a happily married Prima Sai?" Kyani folded her arms, trying not to sound too upset in front of Stevan.

"I…" Kyna sighed. "Yeah, I guess I better."

"I probably should head back too, I need to make sure our Prime Sai is alright."

Kyani turned to him, hesitant at first, but asked anyway, "Will I…see you again?" Her question made Kyna turn and look at them with a soft knowing smile.

Stevan looked back at her and also smiled, giving her a wink. "You have my word, pretty lady." He then bowed to the group, turned on his heels and headed back towards Esailles Palace.

Kyna grabbed Xurian's arm. "Come on, I'll take you back to Terralyn, since it's near Metayale." She then looked at Red. "Take care of yourself."

Red nodded, watching the two get back in the carriage. "Aren't you going with them, Kyani?"

Kyani shook her head. "Nope. I'm coming with you."

"But."

"No 'buts'. The last thing I'm going to do is let you and that little thief face anything alone." She smiled, putting an arm around Red. "You need a friend now, more than anything."

⁂

As Dymona, Alex and Ambrose came upon the shores of Kaatina, on the back of Cesna, Alex told the two he just wanted to check on things before they crossed through the inita and headed onto Eagali. The two waited on the yaitali, while he disappeared among the crowds of people. About a half an hour later he returned to them, tense and angry. "Dymona, are you able to take him to Eagali on your own?"

Dymona looked up from Ambrose to him and immediately noticed fresh cuts and bruises on his arms, and his lip was busted. "What happened to you!?"

"No time to explain, please, can you take him on your own? I need to take care of something." Dymona nodded, not taking her eyes off his wounds. Alexander noticed the shock and somewhat concern in her eyes and pushed aside his anger for a moment to give her a small smile. "Don't worry about me," he assured her, "I'll be fine." He winked. "We will meet again soon."

Dymona nodded again and smiled back, before realizing it, and without another word, steered Cesna back out into the water. Alexander waited until they were out of sight, before storming back to the palace. He plowed up the marble steps, thrusting the door open wildly with one arm, smacking the unsuspecting illura, who was making his way up to the door, right in the nose.

"YEEOOWCH!" the boy screamed, putting his hand to his nose. Alex didn't even notice, continuing his fast gait through the hallway. Stevan heard the yell and ran through the other side of the hall and up to the boy.

"What happened to you, Amal?" Stevan asked, trying to pry the boy's hand off of his nose. He shook his head and stepped away from Stevan, his mint tinted hair frazzled in his face.

"Alik hif 'e in uh 'ead wif uh duh!" he muttered, his voice muffled under his hand.

Stevan could not resist the urge to chuckle at the answer. "'E 'id?" he teased.

Exodus II

"'Et up!" Amal yelled, taking his free hand and punching the man square in his arm.

Stevan chuckled a bit more and stepped back, "Okay! I'll stop." He laughed. The sudden shatter of glass in the distance jarred both of them. Stevan cringed while the boy jumped, both looking towards the end of the hallway. After a moment of hesitation, Stevan looked away to see a young girl walking across the hall to their left. "Anada! Anada!!" he called.

The girl stopped and turned her head back to them, a minty-green braid hanging from the left side of her face just touching her shoulder. "Yea? What is it?" she asked hastily.

"Take your brother to the infirmary quickly!" he ordered. She looked from him to her brother, who had his hand still glued to his nose, thinking it would surely fall off, if he let go.

"But I was just about to go and *talk* with Kunoki. I've been waiting to all xana!"

"'Ore ike irt wif im," Amal added.

Stevan nudged him to behave. The girl gave her brother a glare as Stevan said, "Now you can't just leave your brother here with a broken nose, can you?"

"Sure can," she said, without a moment's thought. Stevan's eyes narrowed a bit. He was just about to say, "Forget it," and do it himself when the shattering of glass again pierced their ears and they all jumped. Staring down the long hallway, Anada's eyes widened and she hurried to her brother. Grabbing his hand, she pulled him towards the door, "I-I'll take him now," she said, finally prying her eyes away from the hall and back to Amal. Stevan nodded, still a bit shaken. She took her brother and began to head out the door, "Come on, Sphinx, let's go."

"Uts a fincs?" her brother asked, looking towards her.

"You've never read Terrin's journals about Earth? That was a sculpture of a man with a lion's body…" she began. Her brother nodded. "And he said the nose was broken off." She giggled and looked at him.

He glared at her. "Ou Et UP!!!!" he yelled, as she took off in a run. Stevan watched him chase her around the grounds for a moment, before remembering the shattering glass. He took a deep breath, before turning from the window and slowly headed down the hallway. He tucked his hands into his pockets and listened to the sounds of objects hitting the walls, and more glass toppling over. He knew Yeve would have a hissy fit if she saw what he was doing; then again it seemed that she had hissy fits all the time now. Stevan was noticing that everyone appeared to be acting different-ly. Yeve was always a mean woman, but now she was extreme, and Alex was never one to be in a rage like this. As he approached the door leading into his leader's room, he stopped short. Quietly, he put a hand and his ear to the door. He listened, trying to ignore the clashing and shattering noises from inside.

"She's turned my people against me!" Stevan heard from within the room. "I can't believe she'd stoop that low." He heard a fist pound on a table. "Why can't I be like Dymona? I just don't understand my life anymore. Why is it so easy to be myself around her, and so hard to around here? Be myself…" Stevan heard Alex chuckle at this, "I haven't tapped into my true nature since I ac-cepted this throne. Being myself doesn't even seem normal to me." Stevan gently pressed his hand more so on the door and allowed it to move slightly, in hopes that it wouldn't squeak too loudly, and he could see what was going on. Unfortunately, his attempt failed as the door made a loud creak as he pushed it. The room fell silent as they both froze instantly at the sound. With a sweep of his cloak, Alex turned to face Stevan, his eyes full of fury. "What do you want?" he said dryly,

Exodus II

Stevan stammered, "J-Just heard all the commotion. Wanted to m-make sure nothing was wrong."

Alex stared at him, for what seemed to Stevan as an eternity before commanding, "Just get in here and shut the door!" This caused Stevan to look perplexed. "Now!" Alex roared, making Stevan hurriedly step into the room and shut the door. The floor was a mess of broken glass, books and an assortment of odds and ends. The oak table that Alex usually rested his cloak upon was tipped on its side and the flowers Anada would try and dress up the table with were spread all around. Even his bed was a cacophony of balled up sheets. The comforter was lying half on the bed and half off, while the pillows were nowhere in sight. Stevan guessed they must have been under the bed. He looked from the mess back up to Alex who was staring at him. They stood, staring at each other in silence, both waiting for the other to speak first, yet neither one knowing quite what to say.

"What did you hear?" Alex asked finally.

"Just…that she's turned your people against you." Stevan looked puzzled. "But, Sir? Who's Dymona?"

Alex glared silently, then rolled his eyes. "A zavi," he stated.

Stevan remembered what he'd seen in the coin, and now knew why the name was familiar. "Prime Sai, do you have any idea what the Prima Sai has done?"

"Besides trying to ruin my life!?" Alex raged.

Stevan shook his head. "You don't even know the half of it." He looked up at Alex. "I hope what you've done was worth it," he added, halfheartedly.

"What is that supposed to mean? I had my reasons." He turned back to the window, pausing for a moment. "You don't know what I have been through. I told you that there had to be something more, a long time ago. I found it." He turned his head back towards his sentinel. "I found freedom. I found…myself."

"But, Prime Sai that is no excuse to jeopardize all of Esailles!"

"Don't you get it?" he said forcibly, as he glared at Stevan. "It is not about this horrid life any more. You know, as well as I do, that my wife has jeopardized this regency far more than I. I've been a slave to the fate that was thrust upon me, until now. At first I was only amused by this zavi, but now she's helped change my outlook on life and she doesn't even know it."

"Are you saying you've only been pretending all this time?"

"Pretending? No. Going through the motions? Yes. There is a difference. I remained in my position, because I felt it was my duty to lead you. Now I see that, for all I have tried to do, and as much as I have consumed myself with being how my ancestors were, it was still very easy for my own people to betray me, attack me, and care less about the years I've sat on this throne." He turned and walked back towards the window, leaning onto the sill. His voice lowered and became calm. "I do have her to thank for it, and the more I think about everything that has happened, I wonder if I have any other choice. How can I go back to what I was?"

"But she's a zavi, they don't have any emotion outside of their hatred," Stevan said, as he watched his lord, his brow rising. "You haven't fallen in love with her, have you?" There was silence.

"So that's it, is it? You fell in love with her?" Came a womanly voice from the door. Stevan and Alex both turned sharply to see Yeve's slender body leaning on the doorway, eyes frozen in calm fury. "You've been shirking your duty and gallivanting around for what? A secret love affair?!"

Exodus II

Alex narrowed his eyes and stepped in front of Stevan, "You can't be serious," he stated firmly. "You have no right to come at me, when you can't see past Zephyrus!"

"Yeve, please…" Stevan pleaded, poking his head out from behind Alex.

"Shut UP!" she yelled, "This will not go unseen, mark my words." Alex rolled his eyes and pushed past her. She turned angrily and grabbed his hand, yanking him to turn back towards her. "Don't you walk away from me again," she raged. "Do you have any idea what your obligations to me mean? You are my *husband*. Does that mean anything to you?" Alex looked down at her, snatching his hand from her grip and clenching his teeth.

"Playing my wife again today, are we?" he said through his teeth.

"You are supposed to love me and ME alone," she continued.

Alex's eyes narrowed. "I don't think you know what *love* is," he stated, before turning his back to her. He stilled a moment and then tilted his head back at her. "I take that back. You know full well what love is. Love of power, love of jewels, love of fame and fortune, in other words… you don't love ME at all."

Yeve gasped in sarcasm, "You can't mean that."

"Don't be stupid," he said flatly. "You've been after my position and higher status since before we got married. It was you who convinced my father to arrange our marriage even though everyone knew it was a lie. So don't talk to me about love, not unless you find a heart of your own."

She heard the echo of his steps; as he left her standing there; Stevan behind her, his hand covering his mouth. He stopped midway, glancing back at her one final time, uttering a few simple words, "Or is your heart already with Zephyrus?"

Figure 9 - Eva

17 - Forgiveness

"Hurt would love for you to stay grounded, in bondage. Only true forgiveness can give you the wings to soar." Goldenrod. ~<u>Pain in SunGlow</u>

Dymona and Ambrose slowly made their way across Kaatina, as the female zavi wondered how they'd ever make it the entire way alone. She'd been foolish to let Alex believe she could handle it, but didn't want to take him away from whatever had upset him. As she mulled over their fate, she noticed two other people heading the same way. Listening in on the conversation she heard them mention that they were going to Eagali and it gave her an idea. As quickly as the idea formed she dismissed it, Ambrose was right, zavi aren't exactly the friendliest of people. She watched Ambrose as they walked. In her eyes it looked like he was getting worse by the minute and she realized she really didn't have a choice. Flagging the two down, she told them her predicament and asked if she could tag along. Red didn't even hesitate before allowing her to join them, not even worrying about who they were outside of their names. It was an action that made both Ambrose and Dymona more than a little suspicious. But Dymona opted to deal with that once she got him to Eagali.

The group, now consisting of Red, Kyani, Dymona, and Ambrose, made it onto the shores of Eagali a few hours later. Though the other areas Red and Kyani traveled to have some grasses and a few smaller forests, none could compare to this. Trees large as sequoia danced across the landscape and the floor was a wide array of different types of grasses and brush. Wild flowers as tall as a person were thrown about giving the dense foliage sprinkles of color.

Exodus II

"Maybe we should have brought an axe," jested Kyani, "It's going to take some work to get through all this." The group headed into the jungle, watching their step as they went.

When they'd traveled a couple miles inland, Ambrose tugged on Dymona. "Leave me."

"What? Are you crazy? Stop talking like an idiot," she snorted.

Ambrose shook his head, "Dymona, I'm serious." Hearing the tone of his voice, the others moved out of earshot, to give them privacy.

Dymona's eyes fell on him. "I'm not leaving you in this condition."

"I'm a hindrance to you. How much more of a burden will I be when you find the beast?"

She helped him down to a sitting position. "I'll stay with you…"

"No." Ambrose cut her off sternly. "When I said leave me, I meant it. No one will find me here and I will make a way. You need to find the Beast with the others. At least if you acquire some information, the clan may let you return home."

"Ambrose, please don't…"

"Don't get soft hearted on me now. It's not a good look on you." He chuckled, till he started coughing. Reaching into his pocket, he pulled out a folded piece of papyrus and shoved it in her hand. "Do not read that now. If you need to read it, you will know when. For now, just hold on to it. If someone does find me, I don't want them to find that on me."

Dymona just nodded, before remembering something herself. "If you insist, then please take this." She pulled out a dagger with a bright yellow, sun-shaped stone and placed it in his hand.

"Where did you get this?"

Dymona grinned. "Stole it from Zephyrus' room."

Ambrose grinned too. "Now, where could he have gotten this?" He thought for a moment, then noticed Dymona was still staring at him. "Will you stop looking at me like that and get going? They are waiting for you!"

"Are you sure?"

"Get going!"

Dymona stared at him for a long while, in silence, but finally turned away and moved towards Kyani and Red, glancing back at him ever-so often, just to see him shooing her off. The trio made their way out of sight through the brush.

Ambrose leaned back against the tree, staring up at the sky. "Well, if there really is an Exalted One, and if you hear me, let this be my atonement for all the stupid things I've done." Those were the last words he uttered before falling into a deep sleep.

Meanwhile, tired and still very bitter from all the recent happenings in her life, Eva tried to remain compassionate to the flora and fauna around her, though for all she cared, they could very well die at her hands too. She'd gotten to the point where she felt her heart, and the rest of her emotions, were numb. She was also oblivious to the many attempts on her life that Zephyrus was making; for all she knew, no-one even cared that she still existed. On this day, she decided to go cocomel gathering, as her home was running low on food. With basket in hand, she scaled the trees like an agile squirrel, picking the fruits from the branches. She found the wind playing against her fur lifted her spirits and soon she was actually smiling as she leaped from branch to branch. She finally came across the last tree before the clearing where the meadow started and saw a sight that made her drop all the way to the ground, losing most of the cocomels she had gathered.

"Oh my Astria what happened to you?!" she exclaimed dropping to her knees next to Ambrose's collapsed body. At that moment, seeing him like that, every bit of pent up anger and bitterness was shoved to the back of her mind, as were the cocomels she was out there to get. Ambrose opened his eyes wearily and, seeing her, he closed them again quickly; pangs of regret and guilt plaguing his mind. He was now merely in her mercy, and she could very well kill him, if she wanted to. He prepared himself for the worst. "We've got to get you out of here," she said, throwing aside her basket and lifting his arm up over her shoulder.

Ambrose was stunned, "After all I've done to you..." he stammered, his voice barely above a whisper.

"Could you shut up and help me here?! I can't carry you, you know." Ambrose did not have to be told twice, he used her as balance as he lifted his body just enough to walk. They stumbled back through the blanket of trees to the part of the Elia that she called her home. It was secluded in the trees for the most part, but the light of the suns or the moon could still seep through. She laid him down on her bed of large leaves and soft flower petals and proceeded to examine him. "Good heavens..." she whispered, "What happened to you?"

"I... had a slight... rift... with the higher ups," he said, between what, she could tell were painful breaths. She started to slowly peel the back of his armor apart, and was more surprised at what she found. There was hair, blood and who knows what matted together and attached to his armor. His breathing became sharper, and she knew, even as delicate as she was trying to be, pulling off his armor was painful.

"It's ok," she whispered softly. "It's almost off." Once she got it off, she took a look at his back and her eyes widened. Her heart really went out to him, his back was a mess. She looked closely at the dried blood, scars and scabs and her eyes filled with tears. "You…had wings?"

"Yes." He rasped. "They…were ripped off."

"Oh my Astria!" She covered her mouth, tears falling from her eyes. "How could anyone do this?"

Ambrose tried to chuckle, but coughed instead. "Zavi don't care. I found out the hard way."

"Well, I am going to get you fixed up. You can't stay like this," Eva said, moving quickly around her home. Soon she had the dried blood and stains cleaned from his back and the gashes soaking in a special herb mix she'd learned from her sister. She'd also made him a hot meal, after going out and re-collecting the co-comels she'd lost earlier.

Two days passed and he started to feel his strength returning. It was to the point he couldn't hold it in any longer. When Eva passed, he grabbed her arm gently and she looked back at him. "Why?" he stammered, "Why go through all this trouble for me?"

"Because you are hurt," she said, matter-of-factly.

"With all I put you through, you could have just killed me." His eyes lowered. She'd never seen him so, sorrowful; she figured it had to be why she couldn't be mad at him. She thought about her sister, and through all the hurt and tears she forgave her for Xurian's death. Eva never understood how she could look past everything. But it was this, feeling, this overwhelming feeling of compassion that Eva had, that she now knew Rva has as well, that made everything else irrelevant. She smiled, the first time she had in the weeks after the incident.

"It's called forgiveness," she said, nodding her head, and as she said it, her smile actually widened. In her mind and her heart, she truly gave all the hurt, pain, mistakes and regret to The Exalted One and let it go. It was, literally, like a weight was lifted off of her shoulders.

"You don't think I'm using you again?" he asked, letting go of her arm.

Eva shrugged, moving to continue tidying up the room, "You could be."

"I'm not," he grumbled.

"Then why'd you end up right near my home?" she asked with a smirk, pointing the end of her broom at him.

Ambrose leaned back and averted his eyes to the ceiling, "You aren't going to believe me."

"Try me." She dragged the broom over to the bed and sat beside him.

"I…" he started, "remembered the food you brought to our picnic, and since this is the only place I've ventured to, long enough to look around, it was the only place I knew food was…" He gave a long sigh, "Pitiful I know, but true nonetheless."

Eva had stopped listening, after he said picnic, and was staring at him, "You…remembered?"

Ambrose was taken aback by the question. "Uh, yea… why wouldn't I?" He paused, scratching his head. "Honestly, I remember everything we did. Even down to that blasted pink blanket, with all the green leaves on it. You were the only person who ever asked about the 'T' in my last name." He chuckled a bit to himself, as his eyes fell on her again, noticing her now rosy cheeks. "Are you ok?"

"Yes," she gushed.

"Oh, because your face is red. Does it turn that way a lot?" he questioned, never having seen someone blush before.

"Uh, not exactly no." It made her blush more.

Ambrose tilted his head, finding the way she looked at that moment kind of favorable. "It's a … umm…nice look on you?" he once again felt that uncomfortable feeling, the one he didn't know quite what to do with. It made him wonder if Dymona was right.

Eva just smiled, recognizing the attempt at a compliment, "Thank you."

They looked at each other and in that moment time seemed to freeze in place. Being in her care along with the relief of being released from the dungeons gave him a more relaxed outlook on life. He wondered if this is what enjoyment was. He suddenly grinned at her, deciding to give in to the uncomfortable feeling for a moment. Taking her hand he pulled her close to him. Eva was caught off-guard and tumbled into his lap. Ambrose burst into fits of laughter. Eva blushed more, and didn't know what to say, or even if she should get up. He composed himself and shrugged, "Well, this makes it easier, anyway." Before Eva could ask what he meant by it; he put his hand behind her head and moved his face towards hers. Eva tensed, her heart leaping into her throat, and it somewhat surprised her. She just knew she'd long since gotten over her feelings for him. He placed his lips on hers and as they kissed, he was surprised to find that this time… he actually enjoyed it.

18- The Exile

"The Lord is on my side; I will not fear: what can man do unto me?" Psalm 118:6 (KJV)

The hearty group was now just Red, Dymona and Kyani, making their way through the brush and bramble in search of the Beast. Red didn't quite know what she would do when she came face to face with Tentatio again, and didn't much like the thought of putting Kyani or Dymona in danger. Though, outside of that, she was glad not to be alone in her journey. The trio hadn't really said much to each other, with the rest of the group gone there wasn't much left to talk about. All three were lost in their own thoughts. As Red went to move some branches out of the way, she noticed another bright twinkling star hiding there. Reaching, out she went to touch the orb of glowing light and it turned into another large gold coin. The others craned their neck over Red's shoulder wondering what this coin would show. The visions it played were those of Eva taking in and caring for the hurt Ambrose.

"Well, at least he seems to be in good hands," smiled Kyani. "Who's the woman, though?"

"She's Eva," breathed Dymona, denying the sinking feeling in the pit of her stomach, seeing the visions in the coin. "A serenda Ambrose manipulated to create the Beast."

"And now she is taking care of him?" Kyani gave the coin a disgusted look. "I sure wouldn't."

The coin shrank and dropped into Red's hand and she placed it in her pocket with the other one. "So that's how Tentatio was freed." She remembered the horror she felt seeing her protective barriers destroyed. "I guess, if nothing else, we are on the right track then."

"What do you mean?" Dymona asked, trying to take her mind off her feelings.

"It's natural that Tentatio would try and hunt down the being that released it."

"Ah, so it would be headed here."

"Exactly." The group continued on, looking for a place to stay for the night. "I still need to figure out what these coins are."

"Not sure," shrugged Kyani. "They seem to be picking certain events at random."

Red chuckled. "Nothing like this is ever random. There has to be a reason. Why these particular events?"

Dymona shrugged. "All I know is that I'd never expect her to take him in, after what he caused," she added, in an acidic tone.

Red looked back at her for a long time. With her abilities renewed, she became a lot more sensitive to certain emotions. Witnessing Dymona's reactions, clued her in on the state of her heart, and she realized that this zavi was on a path she didn't even know existed for her.

"What?" Her blunt voice made Red realize she was staring.

"Are you the zavi that received the Book of Light?"

Dymona completely lost all train of thought. "Say again?"

"I didn't think a zavi would read that," quipped Kyani. "Learn something new every-"

Red nudged her to be quiet. "Are you the one who prayed and received the book?"

"Yea. But how did you know?"

"I'm head of the Astrians, I keep tabs on a lot of things." She winked. "You'd be surprised what I know." She held out her hand to Dymona. "I know what it is you are seeking. Keep seeking, you will find what you are looking for. The Exalted One will answer." Dymona found her eyes watering, but denied it was happening. "In the meantime, I want to show you something. Take my hand." The zavi looked at Red's hand, but figured she had nothing to lose. She placed her hand in the angel's palm. Red closed her eyes and ran her element of love through her arm to her hand and out. Dymona jumped, suddenly feeling a surge of warmth fill her body and cause tickles in her stomach, like butterflies.

"W-what is this?" she asked, trembling slightly at the foreign feeling.

"That is love."

◈◈◈◈◈◈◈◈◈◈◈◈◈◈◈◈◈◈◈◈◈

For the rest of the week, Stevan was a nervous wreck, pacing back and forth in his room. He continuously tried to talk to his leader, but to no avail. It seemed as though Alex was not talking to anyone. He had locked himself in the back room, ever since the altercation with Yeve. The back room was small, with no source of light. The Esailles used to use the room as a torment chamber, locking a single soul in there for weeks at a time, to watch them go insane. Not much bigger than the average closet, there was just enough height to stand, and barely enough room to crouch on the floor and stretch out. Inside the room, Alex kneeled; his blood shot eyes were closed as he prayed.

What did I do wrong, Exalted One? Why do you forsake me? All my life I have done what was expected of me, married who they chose for me, acted as my ancestors did. Why do they now rebel against me? Because of her? I know that You put her here for a reason; only You could give one a power like no one else. Only

Exodus II

You could restore the heart, that before was nothing but something in the recesses of my mind. Shall I now be exiled from all that I know and all that I am accustomed because of a fate I didn't create? Shall I be the first sacrificed in Your name? Please, forgive me of my sins and I pray that you keep me, guide me and save me wherever I am to end up now. Make a way for me, my One.

He opened his eyes and a single tear tricked down his cheek, oblivious to his senses except for the slight tickle it caused as it ran down his skin and dropped onto the floor. Then in the midst of the stillness, he heard The Exalted One:

There is a place for you. I have a plan for your life. The path is not easy and very well not what you may think, but have Faith in Me and you shall be fulfilled and bring glory and honor to My Name.

On the morning of the exile, Stevan slumped down onto his bed and stared out the small hole in the wall. His hunter green eyes saddened as he watched his own people preparing for the event. Even Anada and her brother, Amal, were a part of the bustle, though he was sure they were helping only out of force. Amal's nose had two bandages on it, which made the shape of a bright white X that was hard to miss, but it was healing quite well. They were carrying the blood veil; a long thin sheet of material made from the hide of a yaitali and dyed a deep crimson color. He knew they were going to hang it from the two pillars that were placed on either side of the entrance into the clan. One pillar would be in front of each greeter's house. The veil symbolized the tainted blood in the clan, and the urgency to cleanse the camp by discarding the tainted soul in exile. As the soul walked under the veil and out of the camp, the veil was said to have soaked up the tainted blood and the clan would remain cleansed as long as that soul did not return.

Stevan had seen them exile people before, but never a Prime Sai. The Exalted One dealt with them Himself, as the two lords that were exiled seemed to leave of their own accord though the marks of exile were clearly on them. The others knew it was the Exalted One's doing, because none of the clan had placed the marks on them.

But this was *his* Prime Sai. Alexander had been the only person to ever believe in him. When he stepped up to the throne, Stevan was given higher responsibilities and more privileges than he could have ever imagined. As he sat there, he thought about these things and realized how much his Prime Sai had done to make his life more rewarding. The thought of him gone and Yeve in his place made Stevan choke. He wouldn't be at the exile; he didn't think that he could bear to witness it, although his room gave a nice view of it anyway.

As the sun went down, a fire was started next to the right pillar as crowds gathered near the entrance of the camp. Two men walked through the crowd, both wearing long crimson robes that covered all their features, including a hood that was drawn near their eyes. One carried a long, dark brown whip and went to stand beside the left pillar. The other took his position behind the fire. Seeing the men, Stevan knew there was no way of stopping her now. She was right, the majority was with her. Then he saw something that made him leap to his feet. It was Anada, dressed in an all-black dress that fit her body down to her knees, where it flared out and trailed behind her. In her hands was a branding iron. His mind reeled; he thought surely that Yeve would do the exile herself. He assumed the torture would be something she would relish. But not Anada, she was innocent, or so he thought. He couldn't figure out whether she was doing it out of force, or will. Usually the one doing the exile was one of will, but Anada would never *want* to cause such pain and humility to another being, would she?

Exodus II

That was his last straw; he turned around, taking a large sack out from under his bed. Packing his few possessions, he tied the sack and hung it on his shoulder. He had always been proud to be part of the Esailles Regency, but now he wasn't so sure. The only one he wanted was his sister. Suddenly, the crazy things she said about his race seemed perfectly logical. Maybe she had been right all along. Then he thought about what Alex had said over and over again about there being more to what he could see, and what he was used to. That too, didn't sound so funny now. All Stevan knew is there had to be better than sticking around and seeing this. There had to be more and he was going to find out for himself. He knew that had to be what Alex was trying to do, so he would finish it. Taking a long brown cloak from his closet, he threw it on, making sure that even his tail was hidden underneath. Pulling the hood low over his head, he slipped out of the side door and hid between the shelters, ducking the eyes of the crowd as he ran through the back of the camp and into the bushes a few yards behind. He hoped no one spotted him, more than likely they were too caught up in the exile to care about one straggler leaving the camp. And even if they did spot him, he didn't feel anyone would have the time to come after him, anyway.

Back at the camp, four men brought out a large, throne chair, glistening with onyx and ruby jewels. It was made out of the same silver stones that adorned the sides of the steps, in the entrance of the palace. Elegant and sturdy, it was decorated to Yeve's own personal preference. The men sat the throne, near the man with the whip, on the left of the entrance of the camp. A few moments later, the crowd parted to either side as Yeve herself made her way through. She wore her most royal gown, one she refused to wear before, because it resembled Alex's royal robe in its snowy white patterning. She had a high collar, attached to a square boat neck top with short renaissance sleeves. The gown billowed out and trailed just a small bit behind her, radiating in hues of deep blue and maroon. She slowly moved towards the throne, a look of pleasure flowing in her face. Taking a seat, she gazed around eagerly as the crowd moved to close the gap between them.

"Let the exile begin!" she smiled to the deafening cheers of the crowd. And, like clockwork, Alexander walked up from the right side, alone and without a shirt on. His head was raised, eyes to the skies, hiding the intense sorrow that he felt. He was the first of his family to be exiled and worse, to be exiled by his own wife. He had to go out with a look of honor, no matter how broken he was inside. His long, black hair was held together in a single braid, while his hands were clasped together behind his back. No guards or restraints were needed because, to be exiled with honor, was the only bit of dignity one could have left in the camp, and to be restrained, stripped what was left of that dignity away. Coming to the front of the entrance he stopped, bowed to Yeve and then turned his back to the crowd, facing the entrance. Yeve grinned and looked at Anada with a slight nod. Anada moved from the entrance over to the fire, handing the iron to the man standing there. The man heated the iron until the brand glowed red and then handed it back to her. With a look of no emotion, she walked from the fire, over to Alex, standing before him only moments before ceremonially walking behind him.

"With this I brand thee with the mark of the Esailles." She spoke and proceeded to thrust the brand to the center of his back. Steam exploded from the touch of it, and Alex's eyes squeezed shut, as he held his breath but he didn't flinch. Amal turned away at the sight, lightly touching his nose. He couldn't believe what his own sister was doing. The burn set in, she pulled the brand away and held it out with her hand, allowing the man behind the fire to retrieve it and quickly move back to his position. Anada then stepped back, so the entire crowd could see Alex's new brand. They cheered once more. She took a deep breath before turning back to face him. The man standing to the left, with the whip then approached and stopped just next to her. Again, without looking at him, she extended her left arm to him, by which he placed the whip and immediately moved back to his position. Now her hand trembled slightly as she took three precise steps away from him. "Alexander Kali Percival: Leader of the Dark Knights, Prime Sai Percival, ninth lord of the Percival family. As by the appeal of the majority, with Lady Sai Percival's approval, you have been proven to house the tainted blood that stains our clan. For this, your soul is no longer accepted in our camp and you must be exiled." A single tear trickled down her face as she took the whip, and with two strong hard strokes to his back, she had made a perfect blistering X through the still hot brand. Blood trickled from the cuts, making small rivers along his spine. She hesitated to speak for a second but forced herself to say the final words, "Now go, and through the veil our clan shall be cleansed. Never shall you return." At her words, Alexander moved towards the entrance steadily, watching the blood veil with his eyes and he walked underneath it, leaving the camp and his life as he had previously known it, behind. His head, stayed high and he never looked back.

19- Honorable

The Sire was furious, knowing that Ambrose was broken out and both he and Dymona were gone. Of course he took out his frustrations on Zephyrus, blaming him for not keeping tight enough security on Ambrose's cell.

"Now they are both gone you idiot!" the sire shouted, as he paced violently back and forth. Turning suddenly, he jerked Zephyrus from the ground and pressed him up against the wall. "If you don't hunt them down and bring them back, dead or alive, I will have your head!" He threw his arm around, sending Zephyrus to the corner of the cave.

"Oi," muttered Zephyrus. "What possibly did that dolt do, to put a hit out on him?" he asked the Sire, as he rubbed his back.

"The only thing you need to concern yourself with, is what I just told you to do, else I might put a hit out on you, too." Threatened the Sire. "Now get out of my sight!"

Zephyrus slumped out of the Sire's quarters and back towards his own, his anger fuming the more he thought about Ambrose, Dymona and Eva. Dwelling on his failures fanned the flames of his hatred, until an uncontrollable fire erupted within him, and he started to change. His hair flared out like static and turned dark, until it mixed with the night sky. His fangs protruded from his mouth, making it look even more grotesque. The blacks of his eyes had yellow-green, cat-like slits in them now and right between his shoulder blades grew two large bat wings with ripped and tattered edges. His entire body enlarged to five times its normal size and he let out a great roar. Zephyrus' anger and hatred were now in control and he left Zavare, on a hunt for Ambrose and Dymona. He figured they would be with Eva, being that is the only place Ambrose really knows for safety. This made him even more anxious, he'd finally kill her, too. It was in this form that the zavi went, on a vengeful hunt. And, this time, he intended not to fail.

Ambrose suddenly sniffed the air, his nose sensing something foul. He stood, lifting his nose into the air. Eva came in the room to find him walking around sniffing, "What is it? Something wrong?" she asked, lightly touching his arm.

Ambrose looked down at her and commanded, "Just stay here." Then he shuffled past her and outside. Still sniffing the air, he moved stealthily through the foliage. Soon he noticed a large, stout silhouette moving towards Eva's home. "Zephyrus..." Ambrose whispered to himself. "Why is he here in Ultima?" he questioned, with a furrowed brow and uneasy twitch of his tail. "He must be looking for me." Ambrose took a quiet step forward, the grass silently bending beneath his feet. He watched the zavi closely as he moved closer towards him.

Ambrose closed his eyes, placing his hand on his temple. He felt his mind call energy to the tip of his tail, as he slowly opened his eyes. They were filled with a deep blue, the same blue hue that now radiated at the tip of his tail signifying the surges of electrical energy. He knew that it was wrong to use a rare zavi ability against the only other one of his clan known to have it, but it was his main line of offense now that he couldn't transform, and there was no time for morals. Zephyrus noticed the flashes of blue, and he turned to face his prey. Just as Zephyrus leapt at Ambrose, he threw his tail around letting blue lightning scatter from its tip and pierce the zavi's skin. Like a magnet, the energy held him in midair; a slave to the electricity. Ambrose shifted his weight onto his back leg so that he swung his tail back, throwing the zavi into the brush behind him.

Ambrose turned on his heels and took off into a sprint over to the brush, after Zephyrus. Zephyrus untangled himself quickly from the branches, with a mixed look of anger and surprise on his face. "How dare you use *our* power against me!" he raged, letting out a piercing shriek, that sucked the lightning energy thrust at him and absorbed it. Taking the sudden surge of dark energy, he thrust it back at Ambrose hitting him in the shoulder and knocking him into the trunk of the tree. "Now you will die like the imbecile you are," he snarled. Ambrose hunched over, trying painfully to pick himself off the ground. Eva wasn't one to stay idle and rushed to follow after him. Hearing the commotion, she followed the sound, climbing high into the trees. When she'd ran down a thick sturdy branch and peered down, she saw Zephyrus. The sight of just how close and huge he was, caused her to slide and lose her balance. She yelped, loud enough for both Zephyrus and Ambrose to hear. "Look what we have here, the main course," hissed Zephyrus turning their attention to Eva, hanging from the branch.

"I told you to stay behind!" yelled Ambrose, in a fit of annoyance.

Zephyrus chortled, "Pitiful creatures. Might as well make this quick!" He pointed his finger at the base of the tree where Eva hung and a beam of electricity flowed from his fingertip, setting the tree on fire. The flames rushed like a brush fire over the branches and the surrounding grasses. Eva hung there, terrified, as she watched the trail of flames rapidly fly up the bark and straight for her. There was nothing she could do. She closed her eyes and silently prayed. The fire reached her and in a whoosh, charred the only escape she had from the blazing fire beneath her feet. The fire ran down the branch she was holding onto and she let go, tumbling towards the raging inferno.

Ambrose groaned and dashed directly into the flames, catching Eva before the flames had a chance to touch her. Zephyrus cackled seeing the two emerge from the flames. Eva could see that Ambrose was badly burned from it as he set her down, but never had a chance to speak. Zephyrus lashed his tail around quickly wrapping it around his neck surging every last ounce of electric energy he had. The energy lifted him high into the air where the crackling of the electricity lit up the night sky. Zephyrus slammed him into the ground. Ambrose tried to move but couldn't. Eva ran and jumped on Zephyrus but he just tossed her off like a rag doll. The massive zavi stood over Ambrose and prepared to give him one final blow. Ambrose used his last ounce of strength to pull the dagger, that Dymona gave him, out and jab it into Zephyrus's chest. Zephyrus deflated, turning back to his normal self, as Ambrose pulled out the blade. And there he fell, once and for all.

Ambrose collapsed from the effort, Eva rushing over to catch him. She kneeled with him in her arms and her eyes began to water. Ambrose smiled and gazed up at her, his body burned bruised and beaten. She could tell he was having trouble breathing. "Don't leave me." She whispered, as tears slid down her cheek.

"Don't cry, Eva." He coughed. "I'm a no good zavi. You don't need me around." He tried to laugh, but coughed even worse.

"Don't say that. I-I do need you." She sniffed.

Ambrose slowly shook his head. "I manipulated you and left you for dead," he wheezed. "At least now I can say…I…I've made amends for it."

"But…I don't want you to go." More tears fell from her eyes, dropping onto his chest.

Ambrose continued to cough. "You're safe now." He closed his eyes taking a moment to softly touch her cheek as she felt more of his weight on her. "And I guess...I guess maybe this...is what love was."

And that was the last word he ever spoke.

⸎⸎⸎⸎⸎⸎⸎⸎⸎⸎⸎⸎⸎⸎⸎⸎⸎⸎

With the moons as his constant guides, Stevan slowly wandered, keeping close to the shadows and only moving when the stars lit the skies. His mind was clouded with thoughts of his Prime Sai and what he would do with himself, now that he had been exiled. Stevan felt that he, too, was exiled since surely he could never hope to return to Kaatina, at least not without punishment. Yeve was a harsh and powerful wife, with a lot of sway, so with her as the self-proclaimed Prime and Prima Sai she would be able to do whatever she wanted. That in mind, he resolved that the last place he would ever want to be, is in Kaatina. He wondered if his sister would let him hide out in Korin, even though he felt like a traitor there too. He decided it was his best bet, so he traveled through the three initas leading to Korin, building himself a small raft to get across the ocean. The entire trip, he felt as though something was wrong. Even for him, wandering by nightfall, he was sure something had to stir sometime. The eerie silence had begun to send cold chills down his back. The flutterbies, with their glow that radiated like the twinkle of tiny stars, had helped give his journey out of Kaatina some cheer and color, but since he stepped foot off of that Inita, the flutterbies were no longer seen. Even the bunniflies, who loved to play follow the people, were nowhere to be found. Nothing moved, no one shuffled, and he didn't hear anyone sleeping. Stevan felt he could have walked in broad daylight and not a soul would see his presence.

Exodus II

When he got to Korin, the scene was not any better. The corrupted land that Red, Kyani and Kyna saw had now spread through most of the inita. As he looked around he noticed a lot of discolorations in the grasses near him. He knelt down to examine the grass more closely and as he touched the blades beneath his feet he realized, there was blood on them. He rose quickly and turned towards Terralyn. Running towards the regency, he hoped that he could find his sister. She had to know what was going on, that is if the blood he had found was not hers. As he reached the huts his heart dropped at the sight. The village was in ruins and there was no one in sight. He began searching for his sister among the wreckage. After hours of looking he slowly walked back the way he came, his head spinning with thoughts of worry, confusion and helplessness. He finally collapsed beneath one of the trees. Close to sleep, Stevan suddenly heard rustling in the top of the tree he was sitting under. Shooting bolt upright, he bumped his head hard on the trunk of the tree. Now he was wide awake. Rubbing his head he looked up into the top of the tree, placing his other hand on Cynther, his dagger.

"Is that you?" came a whisper from the tree top.

Stevan looked perplexed. "Trees can talk?" he asked himself out loud, still trying to peer between the branches.

"No stupid," came the answer and then a head popped out from the branches. "What are you doing here?"

"Eshe!" he exclaimed, "Uh... What are you doing in a tree?" he asked as he watched her slowly climb down.

"Hiding. You haven't seen the huge monster running around?" she asked, looking at him quizzically.

"No. What are you talking about? It's been barren all the way from the shore to here, as far as I can tell." He shrugged. "Haven't seen a soul."

She looked at him for a long moment, "You mean Kaatina hasn't been attacked?"

"Not unless it happened after I left. Now will you tell me what in the world is going on?!" he said, slightly irritated.

"Not So Loud!" she protested, slowly opening the hands that had been clasped carefully together, since she climbed out of the tree. "You'll scare her." She revealed a baby bunnifly, whose entire body was shaking. Her bright blue eyes were wide and alert. "She saw her family die with a single swipe. Poor thing is petrified." Eshe glanced over at her brother. "I don't know what it was. It was huge though, towering higher than anything I've ever seen before. Said it was looking for someone. Everywhere it went, the life of the land around it was sucked up into it, leaving nothing but barren wasteland in its wake."

"That would explain the silence. Are all the others in the regency…dead?"

"No, a few escaped but the town is nothing but ruins, I don't know where they went off to." Eshe answered.

Stevan peered over to see into his sister's hands. "She is so little…" he grinned.

"Yeah, and she has no family now." She sighed, as her eyes went to the bunnifly again.

"Sure she does. She has you." Stevan smiled.

"Not if that monster gets to me first." She shuddered, and her brother put his arms around her.

"I won't let anything harm you. Don't you worry!"

"What makes you so sure you can protect me?" she smirked, as the two sat under the bare tree.

Exodus II

"Because…a friend of mine is out hunting that monster." He gave a cheesy grin.

Eshe raised a brow, "Your friend? Don't tell me your regency…"

"No, no…" he stopped her and took her hands in his, still largely grinning, "Sister…I just want to say I'm sorry."

Eshe was only growing more suspicious. "Sorry for what? And let me go, I'm not your girlfriend!" She giggled.

Stevan chuckled. "Stop making me laugh! I'm trying to be serious!"

"Not with that goofy look on your face." She poked her tongue out at him.

"Will you quit?"

"OK, OK!" she laughed, then tried to hold a straight face for him, "Continue."

"I wanted you to know that I'm sorry for not believing all those ideals that you do. I've found a lot of truth in them lately." Eshe's eyes bulged and she was speechless. He continued, "I'm not a part of the Esailles Regency anymore." He turned his eyes to the ground. "They… did some things… that I don't approve of. So I left." Eshe started to speak, but he cut her off. "Listen, a lot that you used to tell me about them, I believe you now." He turned to look back the way he had come. "I never want to go back."

"Awe, Snowball! I'm just glad to have my brother back!" Eshe hugged him tightly. "Well, it's just you and I now. We have a lot of catching up to do." She smiled at him and he smiled back. "Like old times. We will explore together. Deal?"

Stevan's smile widened, as he shook his head. "Deal!" At his words, Eshe threw her free arm around him and shook him a bit.

She was overjoyed that she had her brother again, and Stevan had the feeling he should have made this decision a long time ago.

"So where do we go first?" she asked, stretching.

Stevan thought for a moment, before sighing happily and smiling at her, "First, I have to keep my word."

Eshe cocked her head at him, "Oh?"

He grinned. "Yes, I promised someone I'd see her again. And there is also someone I know you'd love to meet."

"Her?" she stressed, nudging him.

He chuckled, "Oh stop, you."

They both laughed, as Eshe stood, "Well, let's get going." She looked down at the bunnifly in her hand. She had finally stopped shaking, "You, me and her. A new life, just the three of us."

"And in that way you will never be alone. I will always be with you." Black

The trio woke up early the next morning, to resume the hunt, though Kyani and Dymona wondered if they would even find the Beast. They were working their way towards the northern coast of Eagali, figuring the Beast would be coming south from Korin or Riverenda. Even though they'd had a good night's sleep, they were worn out on searching. Red noticed her dejected comrades and stopped, turning to them.

"You two go back, there's no reason for you to face this thing with me," she sighed, looking towards the horizon. "This is my fight; it always has been."

Kyani and Dymona looked at one another and contemplated heading back. Dymona, who hadn't really come to fight, but just to gather information, realized she wouldn't be much help. Even with the information she wouldn't be able to return home. Her heart sank again, coming to terms with the fact that she'd only tagged along because Ambrose wanted her to. Now he was in Eva's care and it just didn't seem as important. "I really can't help in this battle, there really isn't any reason for me to be here. I'm going to go back and make sure Ambrose is OK." She paused, knowing that was a lie. "I don't want to be dead weight." She looked to Red, "It was an honor to travel with an angel." She gave a half smile, before turning on her heels and heading back the way they'd come.

The two watched her for a while, before Red glanced at Kyani. "Well, aren't you going?" Though Kyani was just as tired as Dymona and didn't know if she'd be much help either, she decided to keep her word. She smiled at Red. "No, I'm not going. I told you that I wasn't going to let you face it alone and I meant it. Now please don't try and convince me to return." She moved gracefully past Red and continued towards the shore, not waiting for a response. Red was about to catch up with her, when she saw Kyani stop and look back. Her third eye opened and she ran to the southeast, moving vines, bushes and the trees' outstretched hands. She seemed to run through the forest, so swiftly that Red had a hard time keeping up. The more she ran the more it looked as if nothing was in her path at all. Leaping gracefully over the bushes that stood to the side of the entrance of the forest she met the inita's edge and it was there that Red saw why she was running. There towering high above them, was Tentatio. Soon as the Beast spotted them it sent a wave of energy at them both, bowling over them like a strong gust of wind. But it wasn't an energy blast like they expected. As they felt it rush over them a flood of specific memories flashed in their minds. For Kyani, they were replays of her childhood. For Red, they were images of the collapse of Astria and her final moments before the fall. Kyani fell under a trance to her thoughts, the effect of the energy. Red fought against it, rather trying to jog her memory for images of the first fight with Temptation. How she imprisoned it. That part of her memory still wasn't clear, or was it being blocked? Red held her head with both hands, slowly standing against the pull of her memories.

"Stop blocking me!" she screamed through the gusts of energy, moving forward as if struggling through turbulent winds. Then she remembered that her powers were restored. Stopping in the midst of the torrents, she clasped her hands together and brought them up over her head. Red and white sparkles started to swirl up from the ground and all around her, floating wildly in the energy still rushing past. As she parted her hands, a long maroon staff emerged from the condensation of the sparkles. It was thin and curled about the ends. On the tip was a heart with long clear wings coming out of one side, in a fan shape that eventually stopped at the base of the staff. Red grabbed it strong yet gently in the middle and a shield formed out of the tip .Blocking the winds of energy coming at her, she was able to clear her mind enough to try and search for the memories she really needed. When Tentatio noticed her pushing back on it, and no longer under the trance, it started to flee towards the ocean. At the shore, Temptation bulldozed over the waters, causing typhoon-sized waves to crash across the shore.

"You won't get away that easy!" Red yelled, darting off after the Beast as fast as her legs could carry her. Wings sprouted from her back as she reached the shore and she leaped into the air, twisting and turning with speed and grace.

With the whirlwind of energy dispersed, Kyani broke free of the trance and saw the two about to fight in the ocean. Her third eye opened but instead of doing its customary beam of light, it projected the scene in a different way in Kyani's sight. "Red! It's drawing energy from the water!" she shrieked.

Before Red could get a handle on what Kyani was saying, Tentatio threw its arms to the side and spun in the water three times, allowing wisps of energy to drip from its hands and wind around her. Growing thicker on each spin it pushed its hands together, forcing the mass of energy forward, punching Red straight in the stomach. Blood spat from her mouth as she dropped to the ground and slid to a halt on the grass. Reacting quickly, she hauled herself back into the air and tried to also spin and call her own energy, but Tentatio was not only gaining strength but also agility. She soon found herself backsliding into a halt on the grass again, this time face first.

Tentatio cackled "You are too slow," it teased, as it shot high into the air, sending large waves of water chaotically cascading down in its wake. It leaned back so that it twisted as it fell, the energy forming around its limbs and tearing down like a tornado, puncturing Red right in the heart. "Now … die," it spoke, forcing the haze of energy into her. Red screamed. Her eyes shut tightly, as her body convulsed in reaction, as the energy was literally sucking the life out of her. Kyani focused her eye on Tentatio, but the beam of light only bounced back off of the energy field that Temptation built up. Then Kyani watched, as three golden glows appeared around Red, and started rapidly circling her, each one growing in size. She realized it was the three coins Red collected; they were creating a shield which cut through the torrent of Temptation's energy.

Suddenly, a large black mass oozed from the forests, like liquid paint flying in the wind. The pure energy formed the shape of the man Red had become familiar with, even though she had yet to see his face. The sound of his energy and the steadily growing energy of Temptation turned to a rough howl around them as they stared at each other. The air around them seemed to swell, as if the two were the opposite ends of a magnetic pole. The closer they came, the harder it was for them to take another step and the more violently the wind blew. It pressed and pulled at them, tugging and ripping at every corner of their body so much that the force of it, of each other, formed like a barrier drowning out the outside world.

With the faceless man holding Tentatio's energy within his own, and the coins separating Red from the torrent of energy it was sending at her, she was finally able to regain her equilibrium. As she stood, she drew the energy from within herself and her body lifted through the center of the tornado and she allowed it to force her to spin, using the violent thrusts to her advantage. She kicked her legs to make her spin even faster than the energy and she interlaced, merging with a sea of red, the energy from anything and everything around her for miles that represented that color.

The feeling of the waves of energy was greater than the blood flowing through her veins. It was like a thick liquid feeling surging through every part of her.

Temptation, trying to counter what the mass of darkness was doing, kicked the energy into an even more chaotic state and it became ballistic, and uncontrollable. Energy wisps ripped and tore in every direction but it couldn't penetrate the black mass. The faceless man watched in awe seeing Red call her energy and as the energy exploded around her in small sparks, he knew she was shifting it into that of pure love. She'd remembered how to imprison it, by using what she'd always proclaimed was one of the greatest divine powers there is.

The red energy grew bigger and started to surround Tentatio as well, the dark figure taking the hint and halting his own efforts. The sparks that flew from the red energy now were heart shaped and exploded in a puff of sparkles and any of Tentatio's energy the red hearts touched, exploded with it. Red stopped spinning, having turned its tornado into a whirlwind of red, and she looked down at the Beast.

"I don't understand!" Tentatio raged, "How did you?"

"Simple. Love conquers a multitude of SIN. You are the walking recharging station for that multitude of SIN, so in essence, Love conquers you too." Red then stretched her arms out towards Tentatio and the red whirled around and down her arms to bend and stretch over it and then plunge into her, the love overtaking the energy, until beams of red poured out of it and turned into bright red rays of light as it dissipated in a sea of bright red glow. Before the glow disappeared completely along with Tentatio, she heard its voice scream in her mind, "Not imprisoned again!!!!" Red's eyes closed solemnly and she sighed in relief, gazing around.

Exodus II

The chaotic energy left the land and ocean completely dead and still.

Red floated down to rest just above the ground, the three of them seeing just how much of the area Temptation drained of its energy. Red took a moment to let it register the magnitude of the task before her. The huge mass of darkness landed beside her, yet still, not looking in her direction. "I'm here to help you," a soft masculine voice said in her mind. She smiled, realizing the voice was oddly familiar. Her eyes blinked as she focused on the energy she had concentrated. She rested her arms at her side as she turned her gaze up to the sky. Glowing Red light soon radiated through her body. The form of the man collapsed and he moved around her, his shape stretching to fold over her hands almost like holding them. The angel noticed that as her energy flowed out and mixed with his it became pure white. It flooded the ground with a shine that was led with rainbow sparkles. Everything it touched restored the colors of it more vividly than before, as it renewed the life that had been ripped away. The two moved as one, floating higher across the lands and oceans and continued to raise high into the air, returning the beauty of the skies. Colors flashed through the clouds like someone painting with a multicolored paintbrush, sweeping every inch and casting its own magnificence into the lands of Za-nali. It had been healed, both inside and out. The only land that didn't change, was that of Zavare.

As the last bit of energy left her hands, her body dulled in hue. Her energy was fully spent, and with no energy for her own sustenance, her eyes closed, body limped and she fell into the arms of the pure darkness. He floated slowly down with her, enjoying the moment of feeling her warmth and shifting his energy to her, restoring her strength. They landed and he carefully laid her in the grass, making sure he'd completely renewed her strength before letting her go. Before the mass of darkness vanished again, she opened her eyes. For the first time the faceless man stared down into her eyes with his own. As she stared within them she noticed something, they shined in every color imaginable.

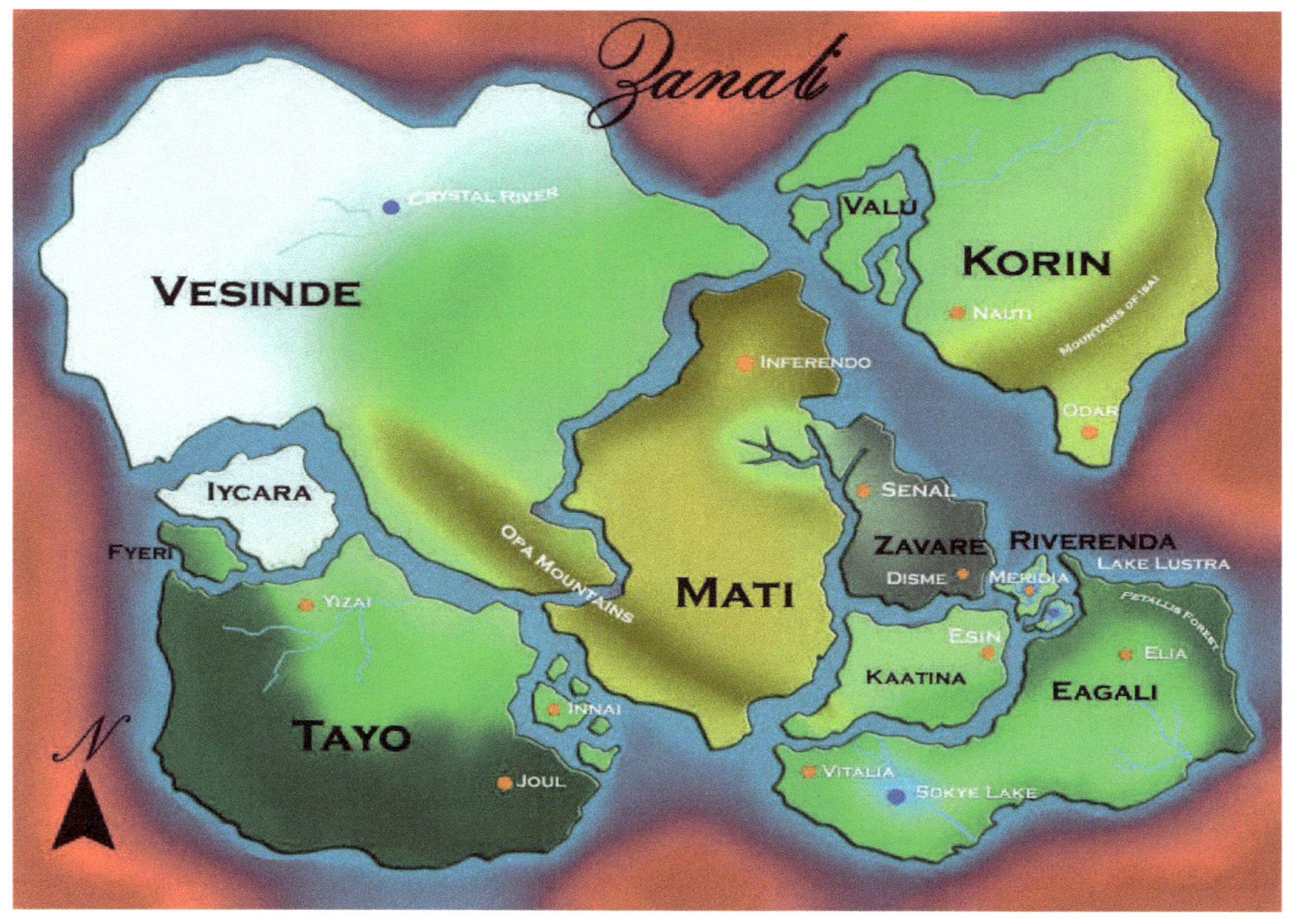

Figure 10 - Map of Zanali